FINDS A WAY

Love
FINDS A WAY

 3 MODERN ROMANCES MAKE FALLING IN LOVE SIMPLE AND SWEET

WANDA &
BRUNSTETTER

BARBOUR
PUBLISHING

For more information about Wanda E. Brunstetter, please access the author's website at the following Internet address: www.wandabrunstetter.com

Cover design: Müllerhaus Publishing Arts, Inc., www.Mullerhaus.net

Published by Barbour Publishing, Inc., P.O. Box 719, Uhrichsville, OH 44683, www.barbourbooks.com

Our mission is to publish and distribute inspirational products offering exceptional value and biblical encouragement to the masses.

 Member of the
Evangelical Christian
Publishers Association

Printed in the United States of America.

CONTENTS

BLUEBERRY SURPRISE

DEDICATION

To my friend Jan Otte, whose sweet treats
have brought joy to so many people.
And to my daughter, Lorine VanCorbach,
a talented musician who has fulfilled
her heart's desire of teaching music.

CHAPTER 1

ain splattered against the windshield in drops the size of quarters. The darkening sky seemed to swallow Lorna Patterson's compact car as it headed west on the freeway toward the heart of Seattle, Washington.

"I'm sick of this soggy weather," Lorna muttered, gripping the steering wheel with determination and squinting her eyes to see out the filmy window. "I'm drained from working two jobs, and I am not happy with my life."

The burden of weariness crept through Lorna's body, like a poisonous snake about to overtake an unsuspecting victim. Each day as she pulled herself from bed at five in the morning, willing her tired body to move on its own, Lorna asked herself how much longer she could keep going the way she was.

She felt moisture on her cheeks and sniffed deeply. "Will

I ever be happy again, Lord? It's been over a year since Ron's death. My heart aches to find joy and meaning in life."

Lorna flicked the blinker switch and turned onto the exit ramp. Soon she was pulling into the parking lot of Farmen's Restaurant, already full of cars.

The place buzzed with activity when she entered through the back door, used only by the restaurant employees and for deliveries. Lorna hung her umbrella and jacket on a wall peg in the coatroom. "I hope I'm not too late," she whispered to her friend and coworker, Chris Williams.

Chris glanced at the clock on the opposite wall. "Your shift was supposed to start half an hour ago, but I've been covering for you."

"Thanks. I appreciate that."

"Is everything all right? You didn't have car troubles, I hope."

Lorna shook her head. "Traffic on the freeway was awful, and the rain didn't make things any easier."

Chris offered Lorna a wide grin, revealing two crescent-shaped dimples set in the middle of her pudgy cheeks. Her light brown hair was pulled up in a ponytail, which made her look less like a woman of thirty-three and more like a teenager. Lorna was glad her own hair was short and naturally curly. She didn't have to do much, other than keep her blond locks clean, trimmed, and combed.

"You know Seattle," Chris said with a snicker. "Weather-wise, it wasn't much of a summer, was it? And now fall is just around the corner."

It wasn't much of a year either, Lorna thought ruefully. She drew in a deep breath and released it with a moan. "I am so tired—of everything."

"I'm not surprised." Chris shook her finger. "Work, work, work. That's all you ever do. Clerking at Moore's Mini-Mart during the day and working as a waitress here at night. There's no reason for you to be holding down two jobs now that. . ." She broke off her sentence. "Sorry. It's none of my business how you spend your time. I hate to see you looking so sad and tired, that's all."

Lorna forced a smile. "I know you care, Chris, and I appreciate your concern. You probably don't understand this, but I need to keep busy. It's the only way I can cope with my loss. If I stay active, I don't have time to think or even feel."

"There are other ways to keep busy, you know," Chris reminded her.

"I hope you're not suggesting I start dating again. You know I'm not ready for that." Lorna pursed her lips as she slowly shook her head. "I'm not sure I'll ever be ready to date, much less commit to another man."

"I'm not talking about dating. There are other things in life besides love and romance. Just ask me—the Old Maid of the West." Chris blinked her eyelids dramatically and wrinkled her nose.

Lorna chuckled, in spite of her dour mood, and donned her red and blue monogrammed Farmen's apron. "What would you suggest I do with my time?"

"How about what you've always wanted to do?"

"And that would be?"

"Follow your heart. Go back to school and get your degree."

Lorna frowned. "Oh, that. I've put my own life on hold so long, I'm not sure I even want college anymore."

"Oh, please!" Chris groaned. "How many times have I heard you complain about having to give up your dream of teaching music to elementary school kids?"

Lorna shrugged. "I don't know. Dozens, maybe."

Chris patted her on the back. "Now's your chance for some real adventure."

Lorna swallowed hard. She knew her friend was probably right, but she also knew going back to school would be expensive, not to mention the fact that she was much older now and would probably feel self-conscious among those college kids. It would be an adventure all right. Most likely a frightening one.

"Think about it," Chris whispered as she headed for the dining room.

"I'll give it some thought," Lorna said to her friend's retreating form.

Evan Bailey leaned forward in his chair and studied the recipe that had recently been posted online. "Peanut butter and chocolate chip cookies. Sounds good to me." He figured Cynthia Lyons, his online cooking instructor, must like desserts. Yesterday she'd listed a recipe for peach cobbler, the day before that it was cherries jubilee, and today's sweet treat was

his all-time favorite cookie.

Evan was glad he'd stumbled onto the website, especially since learning to cook might fit into his plans for the future.

He hit the PRINT button and smiled. For the past few years he'd been spinning his wheels, not sure whether to make a career of the air force or get out at the end of his tour and go back to college. He was entitled to some money under the GI Bill, so he had finally decided to take advantage of it. Military life had its benefits, but now that Evan was no longer enlisted, he looked forward to becoming a school guidance counselor, or maybe a child psychologist. In a few weeks he would enroll at Bay View Christian College and be on his way to meeting the first of his two goals.

Evan's other goal involved a woman. He had recently celebrated his twenty-eighth birthday and felt ready to settle down. He thought Bay View would offer him not only a good education, but hopefully a sweet, Christian wife as well. He closed his eyes, and visions of a pretty soul mate and a couple of cute kids danced through his head.

Caught up in his musings, Evan hadn't noticed that the paper had jammed in his printer until he opened his eyes again. He reached for the document and gritted his teeth when he saw the blinking light, then snapped open the lid. "I think I might need a new one of these to go along with that wife I'm looking for." He pulled the paper free and chuckled. "Of course, she'd better not be full of wrinkles, like this pitiful piece of paper."

Drawing his gaze back to the computer, Evan noticed

on the website that not only was Cynthia Lyons listing one recipe per day, but beginning tomorrow, she would be opening her chat room to anyone interested in discussing the dos and don'ts of making sweet treats. Her note mentioned that the participants would be meeting once a week at six o'clock Pacific standard time.

"Good. It's the same time zone as Seattle. Wonder where she lives?" Evan positioned his cursor over the sign-up list and hit ENTER. Between the recipes Cynthia posted regularly and the online chat, he was sure he'd be cooking up a storm in no time at all.

When Lorna arrived home from work a few minutes before midnight, she found her mother-in-law in the living room, reading a book.

"You're up awfully late," Lorna remarked, taking a seat on the couch beside Ann.

"I was waiting for you," the older woman answered with a smile. "I wanted to talk to you about something."

"Is anything wrong?"

"Everything here is fine. It's you I'm worried about," Ann said, squinting her pale green eyes.

"What do you mean?"

"My son has been dead for over a year, and you're still grieving." A look of concern clouded Ann's face. "You're working two jobs, but there's no reason for it anymore. You have a home here for as long as you like, and Ed and I ask

nothing in return." She reached over and gave Lorna's hand a gentle squeeze. "You shouldn't be wearing yourself out for nothing. If you keep going this way, you'll get sick."

Lorna sank her top teeth into her bottom lip so hard she tasted blood. This was the second lecture she'd had in one evening, and she wasn't in the mood to hear it. She loved Ron's parents as if they were her own. She'd chosen to live in their home after his death because she thought it would bring comfort to all three of them. Lorna didn't want hard feelings to come between them, and she certainly didn't want to say or do anything that might offend this lovely, gracious woman.

"Ann, I appreciate your concern," Lorna began, searching for words she hoped wouldn't sound harsh. "I am dealing with Ron's death the best way I can, but I'm not like you. I can't be content to stay home and knit sweaters or crochet lacy tablecloths. I have to keep busy outside the house. It keeps me from getting bored or dwelling on what can't be changed."

"Busy is fine, but you've become a workaholic, and it's not healthy—mentally or physically." Ann adjusted her metal-framed reading glasses so they were sitting correctly on the bridge of her nose. "Ed and I love you, Lorna. We think of you as the daughter we never had. We only want what's best for you." Her short, coffee-colored hair was peppered with gray, and she pushed a stray curl behind her ear.

"I love you both, and I know you have my welfare in mind, but I'm a big girl now, so you needn't worry." Lorna knew her own parents would probably be just as concerned for her well-being if she were living with them. She was almost thankful

Mom and Dad lived in Minnesota, because she didn't need two sets of doting parents right now.

"Ed and I don't expect you to give up your whole life for us," Ann continued, as though Lorna hadn't spoken on her own behalf. "You moved from your home state to attend college here; then shortly after you and Ron married, you dropped out of school so you could work and pay his way. Then you kept on working after he entered med school, in order to help pay all the bills for his schooling."

Lorna didn't need to be reminded of the sacrifices she'd made. She was well aware of what she'd given up for the man she loved. "I'm not giving up my life for anyone now," she said as she sighed deeply and pushed against the sofa cushion. Ann didn't understand the way she felt. No one did.

"Have you considered what you might like to do with the rest of your life?" her mother-in-law persisted. "Surely you don't want to spend it working two jobs and holding your middle-aged in-laws' hands."

Lorna blinked back sudden tears that threatened to spill over. She used to think she and Ron would grow old together and have a happy marriage like his parents and hers did. She'd imagined them having children and turning into a real family after he became a physician, but that would never happen now. Lorna had spent the last year worried about helping Ron's parents deal with their loss, and she'd continued to put her own life on hold.

She swallowed against the lump in her throat. It didn't matter. Her hopes and dreams died the day Ron's body was

lowered into that cold, dark grave.

She wrapped her arms around her middle and squeezed her eyes shut. Was it time to stop grieving and follow her heart? Could she do it? Did she even want to anymore?

"I've been thinking," Ann said, breaking into Lorna's troubling thoughts.

"What?"

"When you quit school to help pay our son's way, you were cheated out of the education you deserved. I think you should go back to college and get that music degree you were working toward."

Lorna stirred uneasily. First Chris, and now Ann? What was going on? Was she the victim of some kind of conspiracy? She extended her legs and stretched like a cat. "I'm tired. I think I'll go up to bed."

Before she stood up, Lorna touched her mother-in-law's hand. "I appreciate your suggestion, and I promise to sleep on the idea."

" 'Take delight in the Lord, and he will give you the desires of your heart,' " Ann quoted from the book of Psalms. "God is always full of surprises."

Lorna nodded and headed for the stairs. A short time later, she entered her room and flopped onto the canopy bed with a sigh. She lay there a moment, then turned her head to the right so she could study the picture sitting on the dresser across the room. It was taken on her wedding day, and she and Ron were smiling and looking at each other as though they had their whole lives ahead of them. How happy they'd been back then—full of hope and dreams for their future.

A familiar pang of regret clutched Lorna's heart as she thought about the plans she'd made for her own life. She'd given up her heart's desire in order to help Ron's vision come true. Now they were both gone—Ron, as well as Lorna's plans and dreams.

With the back of her hand, she swiped at an errant tear running down her cheek. *Help me know what to do, Lord. Could You possibly want me to go back to school? Can I really have the desires of my heart? Do You have any pleasant surprises ahead for me?*

CHAPTER 2

"What did the ground say to the rain?" Lorna asked an elderly man as she waited on his table.

He glanced out the window at the pouring rain and shrugged. "You got me."

"If you keep this up, my name will be mud!" Lorna's laugh sounded forced, but it was the best she could do, considering how hard she'd had to work at telling the dumb joke.

"That was really lame," Chris moaned as she passed by her table and jabbed Lorna in the ribs.

The customer, however, laughed at Lorna's corny quip. She smiled. *Could mean another nice tip.*

She moved to the next table, preparing to take an order from a young couple.

"I'll have one of the greasiest burgers you've got, with a

side order of artery-clogging french fries." The man looked up at Lorna and winked.

Offering him what she hoped was a pleasant smile, Lorna wrote down his order. Then she turned to the woman and asked, "What would you like?"

"I'm trying to watch my weight," the slender young woman said. "What have you got that tastes good and isn't full of fat or too many calories?"

"You don't look like you need to worry about your weight at all." Lorna grinned. "Why, did you know that diets are for people who are thick and tired of it all?"

The woman giggled. "I think I'll settle for a dinner salad and a glass of unsweetened iced tea."

When Lorna turned in her order, she bumped into Chris, who was doing the same.

"What's with you tonight?" her friend asked.

"What do you mean?"

"I've never seen you so friendly to the customers before. And those jokes, Lorna. Where did you dig them up?"

Lorna shrugged. "You're not the only one who can make people laugh, you know. I'll bet my tips will be better than ever tonight."

"Tips? Is that what you're trying to do—get more tips?"

"Not necessarily more. Just bigger ones." As she spoke the words, Lorna felt a pang of guilt. She knew it wasn't right to try to wangle better tips. The motto at Farmen's was to be friendly and courteous to all customers. Besides, it was the Christian way, and Lorna knew better than to do anything

other than that. She'd gotten carried away with the need to make more money in less time. *Forgive me, Father,* she prayed.

Chris moved closer to Lorna. "Let me see if I understand this right. You're single, living rent free with your in-laws, working two jobs, and you need more money? What gives?"

"I've given my notice at the Mini-Mart," Lorna answered. "Next Friday will be my last day."

Chris's mouth dropped open, and she sucked in her breath. "You're kidding!"

"I'm totally serious. I'll only be working at this job from now on."

"You don't even like waiting tables," Chris reminded. "Why would you give up your day job to come here every evening and put up with a cranky boss and complaining customers? If you want to quit a job, why not this one?"

"I decided to take your advice," Lorna replied.

"My advice? Now that's a first. What, might I ask, are you taking my advice on?"

"One week from Monday I'll be registering for the fall semester at Bay View Christian College."

Chris's eyes grew large, and Lorna gave her friend's red and blue apron a little tug. "Please don't stand there gaping at me—say something."

Chris blinked as though she were coming out of a trance. "I'm in shock. I can't believe you're actually going back to college, much less doing it at my suggestion."

Lorna wrinkled her nose. "It wasn't solely because of your prompting."

"Oh?"

"Ann suggested it the other night, too, and I've been praying about it ever since. I feel it's something I should do."

Chris grabbed Lorna in a bear hug. "I'm so happy for you."

"Thanks." Lorna nodded toward their boss, Gary Farmen, who had just walked by. "Guess we should get back to work."

"Right." Chris giggled. "We wouldn't want to be accused of having any fun on the job, now, would we?"

Lorna started toward the dining room.

"One more thing," Chris called after her.

"What's that?" Lorna asked over her shoulder.

"I'd find some better jokes if I were you."

The distinctive, crisp scent of autumn was in the air. Lorna inhaled deeply as she shuffled through a pile of freshly fallen leaves scattered around the campus of Bay View Christian College.

Today she would register for the fall semester, bringing her one step closer to realizing her dream of teaching music. The decision to return to school had been a difficult one. Certainly she was mature enough to handle the pressures that would come with being a full-time student, but she worried about being too mature to study with a bunch of kids who probably didn't have a clue what life was all about.

By the time Lorna reached the front door of the admissions office, her heart was pounding so hard she was sure everyone within earshot could hear it. Her knees felt weak and shaky,

and she wondered if she would be able to hold up long enough to get through this process.

She'd already filled out the necessary paperwork for pre-admission and had even met with her adviser the previous week. Today was just a formality. Still, the long line forming behind the desk where she was to pick up her course package made her feel ill at ease.

Lorna fidgeted with the strap of her purse and felt relief wash over her when it was finally her turn.

"Name?" asked the dark-haired, middle-aged woman who was handing out the packets.

"Lorna Patterson. My major is music education."

The woman thumbed through the alphabetized bundles. A few seconds later, she handed one to Lorna. "This is yours."

"Thanks," Lorna mumbled. She turned and began looking through the packet, relieved when she saw that the contents confirmed her schedule for this semester.

Intent on reading the program for her anatomy class, Lorna wasn't watching where she was going. With a sudden jolt, she bumped into someone's arm, and the entire bundle flew out of her hands. Feeling a rush of heat creep up the back of her neck, Lorna dropped to her knees to retrieve the scattered papers.

"Sorry. Guess my big bony elbow must have gotten in your way. Here, let me help you with those."

Lorna looked up. A pair of clear blue eyes seemed to be smiling at her. The man those mesmerizing eyes belonged to must be the owner of the deep voice offering help. She fumbled with the uncooperative papers, willing her fingers to stop shaking. *What is wrong with me? I'm acting like a clumsy fool this morning.* "Thanks, but I can manage," she squeaked.

The young man nodded as he got to his feet, and her cheeks burned hot under his scrutiny.

Lorna quickly gathered up the remaining papers and stood. *He probably thinks I'm a real klutz. So much for starting out the day on the right foot.*

The man opened his mouth as if to say something, but Lorna hurried away. She still had to go to the business office and take care of some financial matters. Then she needed to find the bookstore and locate whatever she'd be needing, and finally the student identification desk to get her ID card. There would probably be long lines everywhere.

Lorna made her way down the crowded hall, wondering how many more stupid blunders she might make before the day was over. She'd been away from college so long; it was obvious she no longer knew how to function. Especially in the presence of a good-looking man.

Evan hung his bicycle on the rack outside his lake-view apartment building and bounded up the steps, feeling rather pleased with himself. He'd enrolled at Bay View Christian College today, taken a leisurely bike ride around Woodland Park, and now was anxious to get home and grab a bite to eat. After supper he'd be going online to check out Cynthia Lyons's cooking class again. Maybe he'd have better luck with

today's recipe than he had last week. Evan's peanut butter chocolate chip cookies turned out hard as rocks, and he still hadn't figured out what he'd done wrong. He thought he'd followed Cynthia's directions to the letter, but apparently he'd left out some important ingredient. He probably should try making them again.

As soon as Evan entered his apartment, he went straight to the kitchen and pulled a dinner from the freezer, then popped it into the oven.

"If I learn how to cook halfway decent, it might help find me a wife," he murmured. "Not only that, but it would mean I'd be eating better meals while I wait for that special someone."

While the frozen dinner heated, Evan went to the living room, where his computer sat on a desk in the corner. He booted it up, then went back to the kitchen to fix a salad. At least that was something he could do fairly well.

"I should have insisted Mom teach me how to cook," he muttered.

As Evan prepared the green salad, his thoughts turned toward home. He'd grown up in Moscow, Idaho, and that's where his parents and two older sisters still lived with their families. Since Evan was the youngest child and the only boy in the family, he'd never really needed to cook. His sisters, Margaret and Ellen, had always helped Mom in the kitchen, and they used to say Evan was just in the way if he tried to help out. So when Evan went off to college, he lived on fast food and meals that were served in the school's cafeteria. When he dropped out of college to join the air force, all of his meals were provided, so again he had no reason to cook.

Now Evan was living in Seattle, attending the Christian college a friend had recommended. He probably could have lived on campus and eaten whatever was available, but he'd chosen to live alone and learn to cook. He'd also decided it was time to settle down and look for a Christian woman.

Evan sliced a tomato and dropped the pieces into the salad bowl. "First order of business—learn to cook. Second order—find a wife!"

Over the last few days, Lorna's tips from the restaurant had increased, and she figured it might have something to do with the fact that she'd given up telling jokes and was being pleasant and friendly, without any ulterior motives.

"I see it's raining again," Chris said as she stepped up beside Lorna.

Lorna grabbed her work apron and shrugged. "What else is new? We're living in Washington—the Evergreen State, remember?"

Chris lifted her elbow, let it bounce a few times, then connected it gently to Lorna's rib cage. "You're not planning to tell that silly joke about the ground talking to the rain again, I hope."

Lorna shook her head. "I've decided to stick to business and leave the humorous stuff to real people like you."

Chris raised her dark eyebrows, giving Lorna a quizzical look. "*Real* people? What's that supposed to mean?"

"It means you're fun-loving and genuinely witty." Lorna frowned. "You don't have to tell stale jokes in order to make people smile. Everyone seems drawn to your pleasant personality."

"Thanks for the compliment," Chris said with a nod. "I think you sell yourself short. You're talented, have gorgeous, curly blond hair, and you're blessed with a genuine, sweet spirit." She leaned closer and whispered, "Trouble is, you keep it hidden, like a dark secret you don't want anyone to discover."

Lorna moved away, hoping to avoid any more of her friend's psychoanalyzing, but Chris stepped in front of her, planting both hands on her wide hips. "I'm not done yet."

Lorna squinted her eyes. "It's obvious that you're not going to let me go to work until I hear you out."

Chris's smile was a victorious one. "If you would learn to relax and quit taking life so seriously, people would be drawn to you."

Lorna groaned. "I want to, Chris, but since Ron's death, life has so little meaning for me."

"You're still young and have lots to offer the world. Don't let your heart stay locked up in a self-made prison."

"Maybe going back to school will help. Being around kids who are brimming over with enthusiasm and still believe life holds nothing but joy might rub off on me."

"I think most college kids are smart enough to know life isn't always fun and games," Chris said in a serious tone. "I do believe you're right about one thing though."

"What's that?"

"Going back to school will be good for you."

CHAPTER 3

Lorna settled herself into one of the hard-backed auditorium seats and pulled a notebook and pen from her backpack. Anatomy was her first class of the day. She wanted to be ready for action, since this course had been suggested by one of the advisers. It would help her gain a better understanding of proper breathing and the body positions involved in singing.

She glanced around, noticing about fifty other students in the room. Most of them were also preparing to take notes.

A tall, middle-aged man, who introduced himself as Professor Talcot, announced the topic of the day—"Age-Related Changes."

Lorna was about to place her backpack on the empty seat next to her when someone sat down. She glanced over and was greeted with a friendly smile.

Oh no! It's that guy I bumped into the other day during registration.

She forced a return smile, then quickly averted her attention back to the professor.

"I'm late. Did I miss much?" the man whispered as he leaned toward Lorna.

"He just started." She kept her gaze straight ahead.

"Okay, thanks."

Lorna was grateful he didn't say anything more. She was here to learn, not to be distracted by some big kid who should have been on time for his first class of the day.

"Everyone, take a good look at the seat you're in," Professor Talcot said. "That's where you will sit for the remainder of the semester. My assistant will be around shortly to get your names and fill out the seating chart."

Lorna groaned inwardly. If she'd known she would have to stay in this particular seat all semester, she might have been a bit more selective. Of course, she had no way of knowing an attractive guy with gorgeous blue eyes and a winning smile was going to flop into the seat beside her.

I can handle this. After all, it's only one hour a day. I don't even have to talk to him if I don't want to.

"Name, please?"

Lorna was jolted from her thoughts when a studious-looking man wearing metal-framed glasses tapped her on the shoulder.

She turned her head and realized he was standing in the row behind, leaning slightly over the back of her seat, holding a clipboard in one hand.

"Lorna Patterson," she whispered.

"What was that? I couldn't hear you."

The man sitting next to Lorna turned around. "She said her name is Lorna Patterson. Mine's Evan Bailey."

"Gotcha!" the aide replied.

Lorna felt the heat of embarrassment rush to her cheeks. *Great! He not only saw how clumsy I was the other day; now he thinks I can't even speak for myself. I must appear to be pretty stupid.*

As she turned her attention back to the class, Lorna caught the tail end of something the professor had said. Something about a group of five. *That's what I get for thinking when I should be listening. Maybe I wasn't ready to come back to college after all.* She turned to Evan and reluctantly asked, "What did the professor say?"

"He said he's about to give us our first assignment, and we're supposed to form into groups of five." A smile tugged at the corners of his mouth. "Would you like to be in my group?"

Lorna shrugged. She didn't know anyone else in the class. Not that she knew Evan. She'd only met him once, and that wasn't under the best of circumstances.

Evan Bailey was obviously more outgoing than she, for he was already rounding up three other people to join their group—two young men and one woman, all sitting in the row ahead of them.

"The first part of this assignment will be to get to know each other," Professor Talcot told the class. "Tell everyone in

your group your name, age, and major."

Lorna felt a sense of dread roll over her, like turbulent breakers lapping against the shore.

It's bad enough that I'm older than most of these college kids. Is it really necessary for me to reveal my age?

Introductions were quickly made, and Lorna soon learned the others in the group were Jared, Tim, and Vanessa. All but Evan and Lorna had given some information about themselves.

"You want to go first?" Evan asked, looking at Lorna.

"I—uh—am in my junior year, and I'm majoring in music ed. I hope to become an elementary school music teacher when I graduate."

"Sounds good. How about you, Evan?" Tim, the studious-looking one, asked.

Evan wiggled his eyebrows and gave Lorna a silly grin. "I'm lookin' for a mother for my children."

"You have kids?" The question came from Vanessa, who had long red hair and dark brown eyes, which she'd kept focused on Evan ever since they'd formed their group.

He shook his head. "Nope, not yet. I'm still searching for the right woman to be my wife. I need someone who loves the Lord as much as I do." Evan's eyebrows drew together. "Oh yeah—it might be good if she knows how to cook. I'm in the process of learning, but so far all my recipes have flopped."

Vanessa leaned forward and studied Evan more intently. "Are you majoring in home economics?"

Evan chuckled. "Not even close. My major is psychology,

but I've recently signed up for an online cooking class." He smiled and nodded at Lorna instead of Vanessa. "You married?"

Lorna shook her head. "I'm not married now." She hesitated then looked away. "My husband died."

"Sorry to hear that," Evan said in a sincere tone.

"Yeah, it's a shame about your husband," Jared agreed.

There were a few moments of uncomfortable silence; then Evan said, "I thought I might bring some sweet treats to class one of these days and share them with anyone willing to be my guinea pig."

Vanessa smacked her lips and touched the edge of Evan's shirtsleeve. "I'll be looking forward to that."

"It's time to tell our ages. I'm twenty-one," Tim said.

Vanessa smiled and said she was also twenty-one.

Jared informed the group that he was twenty-four.

"Guess that makes me the old man of our little assemblage. I'm heading downhill at the ripe old age of twenty-eight," Evan said with a wink in Lorna's direction.

With the exception of Evan, they're all just kids, she thought. *And even he's four years younger than me.*

Vanessa nudged Lorna's arm with the eraser end of her pencil. "Now it's your turn."

Lorna stared at the floor and mumbled, "I'm thirty-two."

Jared let out a low whistle. "Wow, you're a lot older than the rest of us."

Lorna slid a little lower in her chair. *As if I needed to be reminded.*

Evan held up the paper he was holding. It had been handed

out by the professor's assistant only moments ago. "It says here that one of the most significant age-related signs is increased hair growth in the nose." He leaned over until his face was a few inches from Lorna's. As he studied her, she felt like a bug under a microscope. "Yep," he announced. "I can see it's happening to you already!"

Jared, Tim, and Vanessa howled, and Lorna covered her face with her hands. If the aisle hadn't been blocked, she might have dashed for the door. Instead, she drew in a deep breath, lifted her head, and looked Evan in the eye. "You're right about my nose hair. In fact, I'm so old I get winded just playing a game of checkers." She couldn't believe she'd said that. Maybe those stupid jokes she had used on her customers at the restaurant were still lodged in her brain.

Everyone in the group laughed this time, including Lorna, who was finally beginning to relax. "The other day, I sank my teeth into a big, juicy steak, and you know what?" she quipped.

Evan leaned a bit closer. "What?"

"They just stayed there!"

Vanessa giggled and poked Evan on the arm. "She really got you good on that one."

Evan grimaced. "Guess I deserved it. Sorry about the nose hair crack."

He looked genuinely sorry, making Lorna feel foolish for trying to set him up with her lame joke. She was about to offer an apology of her own when he added, "It's nice to know I'm not the oldest one in class."

Lorna didn't know how she had survived the morning. By the time she entered her last class of the day, she wondered all the more if she was going to make it as a college student. *This is no time to wimp out*, she chided herself as she took a seat in the front row. *Choir is my favorite subject.*

The woman who stood in front of the class introduced herself as Professor Lynne Burrows.

She's young, Lorna noted. *Probably not much past thirty. I would be a music teacher by now if I'd finished my studies ten years ago.*

"Do we have any pianists in this class?" Professor Burrows asked.

Lorna glanced around the room. When she saw no hands raised, she lifted hers.

"Have you ever accompanied a choir?"

She nodded. "I play for my church choir, and I also accompanied college choir during my freshman and sophomore years." She chose not to mention the fact that it had been several years ago.

The professor smiled. "Would you mind playing for us today? If it works out well, perhaps you'd consider doing it for all the numbers that require piano accompaniment."

"I'd like that." Lorna headed straight for the piano, a place where she knew she'd be the most comfortable.

"If you need someone to turn the pages, I'd be happy to oblige."

Lorna glanced to her right. Evan Bailey was leaning on the lid of the piano, grinning at her like a monkey who'd been handed a tasty banana. She couldn't believe he was in her music class, too.

"Thanks anyway, but I think I can manage," Lorna murmured.

Evan dropped to the bench beside her. "I've done this before, and I'm actually pretty good at it." He reached across Lorna and thumbed a few pages of the music.

She eyed him suspiciously. "You don't know when to quit, do you?"

He laughed and wagged a finger in front of her nose. "Just call me Pushy Bailey."

"Let's see what Professor Burrows has to say when she realizes you're sitting on the piano bench instead of standing on the risers with the rest of the choir. You *are* enrolled in this class, I presume?"

Evan smiled at her. "I am, and I signed up for it just so I could perfect my talent of page turning."

Lorna moaned softly. "You're impossible."

Evan dragged his fingers along the piano keys. "How about you and me going out for a burger after class? Then I can tell you about the rest of my faults."

"Sorry, but I don't date."

He snapped the key of middle C up and down a few times. "Who said anything about a date? I'm hungry for a burger and thought maybe you'd like to join me. It would be a good chance for us to get better acquainted."

Lorna sucked in her breath. "Why would we need to get better acquainted?"

He gave her a wide smile. "I'm in choir—you're in choir. You're the pianist—I'm the page turner. I'm in anatomy—you're in anatomy. I'm in your group—you're in my—"

She held up one hand. "Okay, Mr. Bailey. I get the point."

"Call me Evan. Mr. Bailey makes me sound like an old man."

"Evan, then."

"So will you have a burger with me?"

Lorna opened her mouth, but Professor Burrows leaned on top of the piano and spoke first. "I see you've already found a page turner."

Lorna shook her head. "Not really. I've always been able to turn my own pages, and I'm sure you need Mr. Bailey's voice in the tenor section far more than I need his thumb and index finger at the piano."

Evan grinned up at the teacher. "What can I say? The woman likes me."

Lorna's mouth dropped open. Didn't the guy ever quit?

"You're pretty self-confident, aren't you?" The professor pointed at Evan, then motioned toward the risers. "Let's see how well you can sing. Third row, second place on the left."

Evan shrugged and gave Lorna a quick wink. "See you later."

"Don't mind him," Professor Burrows whispered to Lorna. "I think he's just testing the waters."

"Mine or yours?"

"Probably both. I've handled characters like him before, so we won't let it get out of hand." The professor gave Lorna's shoulder a gentle squeeze and moved to the front of the class.

Lorna closed her eyes and drew in a deep breath, lifting a prayer of thanks that the day was almost over. She couldn't believe how stressful it had been. Maybe she should give up her dream of becoming a music teacher while she still had some shred of sanity left.

As Evan stood on the risers with the rest of the class, he couldn't keep focused on Professor Burrows or the song they were supposed to be singing. His gaze kept going back to the cute little blond who sat at the piano.

He knew Lorna was four years older than he, and she'd made it clear that she had no interest in dating. Still, the woman fascinated him, and he was determined they should get better acquainted. The few years' age difference meant nothing as far as he was concerned, but it might matter to Lorna. Maybe that's why she seemed so indifferent.

I'd sure like to get to know her better and find out if we're compatible. Evan smiled to himself. He would figure out a way—maybe bribe her with one of his online sweet treats. Of course, he'd first have to learn how to bake something that didn't flop.

CHAPTER 4

When Lorna arrived home from school, she found her father-in-law in the front yard, raking a pile of maple leaves into a mountain in the middle of the lawn.

Ed stopped and wiped the perspiration from the top of his bald head with a hankie he had pulled from the pocket of his jeans. "How was your first day?"

Lorna plodded up the steps, dropped her backpack to the porch, and sank wearily into one of the wicker chairs. "Let's put it this way: I'm still alive to tell about it."

Ed leaned the rake against the outside porch railing and took the chair beside her. "That bad, huh?"

She only nodded in reply.

"Is your schedule too heavy this semester?" he asked, obvious concern revealed in his dark eyes.

Lorna forced a smile. "It's nothing to be worried about."

"Anything that concerns you concerns me and Ann. You were married to our son, and that makes us family."

"I know, but I do have to learn how to handle some problems on my own."

"Problems? Did I hear someone say they're having problems?"

Lorna glanced up at Ann, who had stepped onto the porch. "It's nothing. I'm just having a hard time fitting in at school. I am quite a bit older than most of my classmates, you know."

Ann laughed, causing the lines around her eyes to become more pronounced. "Is that all that's troubling you? I'd think being older would have some advantages."

"Such as?"

"For one thing, your maturity should help you grasp things. Your study habits will probably be better than those of most kids fresh out of high school, too. These days, many young people don't have a lot of self-discipline."

"Yeah, no silly schoolgirl crushes or other such distractions," Ed put in with a deep chuckle.

Lorna swallowed hard. There had already been plenty of distractions today, and they'd come in the form of a young man with laughing blue eyes, goofy jokes, and a highly contagious smile.

"My maturity might help me be more studious, but it sure sets me apart from the rest of the college crowd," she said. "Today I felt like a sore thumb sticking out on an otherwise healthy hand."

"You're so pretty, I'm sure no one even guessed you were a few years older." Ann gently touched Lorna's shoulder.

"Thanks for the compliment," Lorna said, making no mention of the fact that she had already revealed her age during the first class of the day. She cringed, thinking about the nose hair incident. "I'd better go inside. I want to read a few verses of scripture, and I have some homework that needs to be done before it's time to head for work."

Lorna stood in front of the customer who sat at a table in her assigned section with a menu in front of his face. "Have you decided yet, sir?" she asked.

"I'll have a cheeseburger with the works."

He dropped the menu to the table, and Lorna's gaze darted to the man's face. "Wh—what are you doing here?" she rasped.

Evan smiled up at her. "I'm ordering a hamburger, and seeing you again makes me remember that you stood me up this afternoon."

"How could I have stood you up when I never agreed to go out with you in the first place?" Lorna's hands began to tremble, and she knew her cheeks must be pink, because she could feel the heat quickly spreading.

Evan's grin widened. "You never really said no."

Lorna clenched her pencil in one hand and the order pad in the other. "Did you follow me here from my home?"

"I don't even know where you live, so how could I have followed you?" Evan studied his menu again. "I think I'll have

an order of fries to go with that burger. Care to join me?"

"In case you hadn't noticed, I'm working."

"Hmm. . . Maybe I'll have a chocolate shake, too."

Lorna tapped her foot impatiently. "How did you know I worked here?"

He handed her the menu. "I didn't. I've heard this restaurant serves really great burgers, and I thought I'd give it a try. The fact that you work here is just an added bonus."

"I'll be back when your order is up." Lorna turned on her heels and headed for the kitchen, but she'd only made it halfway when she collided with Chris. Apple pie, vanilla ice cream, and two chocolate-covered donuts went sailing through the air as her friend's tray flew out of her hands.

Lorna gasped. "Oh Chris, I'm so sorry! I didn't see you coming."

"It was just an accident. It's okay—I know you didn't do it on purpose," Chris said as she dropped to her knees.

Lorna did the same and quickly began to help clean up the mess. "I'll probably be docked half my pay for this little blunder," she grumbled. "I ought to send Evan Bailey a bill."

Chris's eyebrows shot up. "Who's Evan Bailey?"

"Some guy I met at school. I have him in two of my classes. He's here tonight. I just took his order."

Chris gave her a quizzical look. "And?"

"He had me so riled I wasn't paying attention to where I was going." Lorna scooped up the last piece of pie and handed the tray back to Chris. "I really am sorry about this."

Chris laughed. "It's a good thing it went on the floor and

not in someone's lap." She got to her feet. "So what's this guy done that has you so upset?"

Lorna picked a hunk of chocolate off her apron and stood, too. "First of all, he kept teasing me in anatomy class this morning. Then he plunked himself down at the piano with me during choir, offering to be my page turner." She paused and drew in a deep breath. "Next, he asked me to go out for a burger after school."

"What'd you say?"

"I didn't answer him." Lorna frowned. "Now he's here, pestering me to eat dinner with him."

Chris moved toward the kitchen, with Lorna following on her heels. "Sounds to me like the guy is interested in you."

Lorna shook her head. "He hardly even knows me. Besides, I'm four years older."

"Who's hung up on age differences nowadays?"

"Okay, it's not the four years between us that really bothers me."

"What, then?"

"He acts like a big kid!" Lorna shrugged. "Besides, even if I was planning to date, which I'm not, our personalities don't mesh."

Evan leaned his elbows on the table and studied the checkered place mat in front of him. He had always been the kind of person who knew what he wanted and then went after it. How come his determination wasn't working this time? *Lorna*

doesn't believe me. She thinks I've been spying on her and came here to harass her. I've got to make her believe my coming to Farmen's was purely coincidental. He took a sip of water. *Although it could have been an answer to prayer. Somehow I've got to get Lorna to agree to go out with me. How else am I going to know if she's the one?*

A short time later, Lorna returned with Evan's order, and he felt ready to try again. He looked up at her and smiled. "You look cute in that uniform." When she made no comment, he added, "Been working here long?"

"Sometimes it feels like forever," she said with a deep sigh.

"Want to talk about it?"

She shook her head. "Will there be anything else?"

He rapped the edge of the plate with his knife handle. "Actually, there is."

"What can I get for you?"

"How about a few minutes of your time?"

"I'm working."

"When do you get off work? I can stick around for a while."

"Late. I'll be working late tonight."

Evan cringed. He wasn't getting anywhere with this woman and knew he should probably quit while he was ahead. Of course, he wasn't really ahead, so he decided he might as well stick his neck out a little farther. "I'm not trying to come on to you. I just want to get to know you better."

"Why?"

Evan reached for his glass of water and took a sip. How could he explain his attraction to Lorna without scaring her off? "I think we have a lot in common," he said with a nod.

She raised one pale eyebrow. "How did you reach that conclusion?"

"It's simple. I'm in choir—you're in choir. You're the pianist—I'm the page turner."

"I'm not interested in dating you or anyone else."

Evan grabbed his burger off the plate. "Okay, I get the message. I'll try not to bother you again."

She touched his shoulder unexpectedly, sending a shock wave through his arm. "I–I'm sorry if I came across harshly. I just needed you to know where I stand."

He swallowed the bite of burger he'd put in his mouth. "Are you seeing someone else? You mentioned in class that you're a widow, so I kinda figured—"

Lorna shook her head, interrupting his sentence. "I'm a widow who doesn't date."

Evan thought she looked sad, or maybe she was lonely. He grabbed the bottle of ketchup in the center of the table and smiled at her. "Can we at least be friends?"

She nodded and held out her hand. "Friends."

CHAPTER 5

*L*orna awoke with a headache. She had been back in college a week, and things weren't getting any easier. It was hard to attend school all day, work every evening at Farmen's, and find time to get her assignments finished. She was tired and irritable but knew she would have to put on a happy face when she was at work, no matter how aggravating some of the customers could be. One patron in particular was especially unnerving. Evan Bailey had returned to the restaurant two more times. She wasn't sure if he came because he liked the food, or if it was merely to get under her skin.

Lorna uttered a quick prayer and forced her unwilling body to get out of bed. She couldn't miss any classes today. There was a test to take in English lit and auditions for lead parts in the choir's first performance.

She entered the bathroom and turned on the faucet at the sink. Splashing a handful of water against her upturned face, she cringed as the icy liquid stung her cheeks. Apparently Ann was washing clothes this morning, for there was no hot water.

"Ed needs to get that old tank replaced," Lorna grumbled as she reached for a towel. "Maybe I should stay home today after all."

The verse she'd read the night before in Psalm 125 popped into her mind. *"Those who trust in the Lord are like Mount Zion, which cannot be shaken but endures forever."*

"Thanks for that reminder, Lord. I need to trust You to help me through this day."

"I don't see how we're ever gonna get better acquainted if you keep avoiding me."

Lorna sat in her anatomy class, watching a video presentation on the muscular system and trying to ignore Evan, who sat on her left. She kept her eyes focused on the video screen. *Maybe if I pretend I didn't hear him, he'll quit pestering me.*

"Here, I brought you something." He leaned closer and held out two cookies encased in plastic wrap.

Lorna could feel his warm breath on her ear, and she shivered.

"You cold?"

When she made no reply and didn't reach for the cookies, he tapped her lightly on the arm. "I made these last night. Please try one."

Lorna didn't want to appear rude, but she wasn't hungry. "I just ate breakfast not long ago."

"That's okay. You can save them for later."

"All right. Thanks." Lorna took the cookies and placed them inside her backpack.

"I'm going biking on Saturday. Do you ride?" he asked.

"Huh?"

"I'd like you to go out with me this Saturday. We can rent some bikes at the park and pedal our way around the lake."

"I told you. . .I don't date."

"I know, but the other night you said we could be friends, so we won't call this a date. It'll just be two lonely people out having a good time."

Lorna's face heated up. "What makes you think I'm lonely?"

"I see it in your eyes," he whispered. "They're sad and lonely looking." When she made no reply, he added, "Look, if you'd rather not go, then—"

Lorna blew out her breath as she threw caution to the wind. "All right, I'll go, but you're taking an awfully big chance."

"Yeah, I know." He snickered. "A few hours spent in your company, and I might never be the same."

Lorna held back the laughter threatening to bubble over, but she couldn't hide her smile. "I was thinking more along the lines of our fall weather. It can be pretty unpredictable this time of the year."

Evan chuckled. "Yeah, like some blond-haired, blue-eyed woman I'd like to get to know a whole lot better."

Evan studied the computer screen intently. Brownie Delight was the sweet treat Cynthia Lyons had posted on Tuesday, but he hadn't had time to check it out until today. The ingredients were basic—unsweetened chocolate, butter, sour cream, sugar, eggs, flour, baking powder, salt, and chopped nuts. Chocolate chips would be sprinkled on top, making it doubly delicious. If the brownies turned out halfway decent, he would take some on his date with Lorna. Maybe she'd be impressed with his ability to cook. He hoped so, because so far nothing he'd said or done had seemed to make an impact on her. She hadn't even said whether she'd liked the chocolate peanut butter cookies he'd given her the other day. Lorna was probably too polite to mention that they'd been a bit overdone. This was Evan's second time with these cookies, and he was beginning to wonder if he'd ever get it right.

Evan still hadn't made it to any of the online chats Cynthia Lyons hosted. Now that he was in school all day, his evenings were usually spent doing homework.

Oh well. The chats were probably just a bunch of chitchat about how well the recipes had turned out for others who had made them. He didn't need any further reminders that his hadn't been so successful.

Evan hit the PRINT button to make a copy of the recipe and leaned back in his chair while he waited for the procedure to complete itself.

A vision of Lorna's petite face flashed into his mind. He was attracted to her; there was no question about that. But did they really have anything in common? Was she someone who wanted to serve the Lord with her whole heart, the way Evan did?

The college they attended was a Christian one, but he knew not everyone who went there was a believer in Christ. Some merely signed up at Bay View because of its excellent academic program. Evan hoped Lorna wasn't one of those.

And what about children? Did she like kids as much as he did? Other than becoming an elementary school music teacher, what were her goals and dreams for the future? He needed to know all these things if he planned to pursue a relationship with her.

The printer had stopped, and Evan grabbed hold of the recipe for Brownie Delight. "Tomorrow Lorna and I will get better acquainted as we pedal around the lake and munch on these sweet treats. Tonight I'll pray about it."

The week had seemed to fly by, and when Lorna awoke Saturday morning, she was in a state of panic. She couldn't believe she'd agreed to go biking with Evan today. What had she been thinking? Up until now, she'd kept him at arm's length, but going on what he probably saw as a date could be a huge mistake.

"Then again," she mumbled, "it might be just the thing to prove to Evan how wrong we are for each other."

Lorna crawled out of bed, wondering what she should wear and what to tell her in-laws at breakfast. Not wanting to raise any questions from Ann or Ed, she decided to tell them only that she'd be going out sometime after lunch, but she would make no mention of where. Her plans were to meet Evan at the park near the college, but she didn't want them to know about it. They might think it was a real date and that she was being untrue to their son's memory. She only hoped by the end of the day she wouldn't regret her decision to spend time alone with Evan Bailey.

At two o'clock that afternoon, Lorna drove into the park. The weather was overcast and a bit chilly, but at least it wasn't raining. She found Evan waiting on a wooden bench, with two bikes parked nearby.

"Hey! I'm glad you came!"

"I said I would."

"I know, but I was afraid you might back out."

Lorna flopped down beside him, and he grinned at her. "You look great today."

She glanced down at her blue jeans and white T-shirt, mostly hidden by a jean jacket, and shrugged. "Nothing fancy, but at least I'm comfortable."

Evan slapped the knees of his faded jeans and tweaked the collar on his black leather jacket. "Yeah, me, too."

A young couple pushing a baby in a stroller walked past, and Lorna stared at them longingly.

"You like kids?"

"What?" She jerked her head.

"I asked if you like kids."

"Sure, they're great."

"When I get married, I'd like to have a whole house full of children," Evan said. "With kids around, it would be a lot harder to grow old and crotchety."

"Like me, you mean?"

Evan reached out to touch her hand. "I didn't mean that at all."

She blinked in rapid succession. "I am a lot older than most of the other students at Bay View."

"You're not much older than me. When I was born, you were only four."

She grunted. "When you were six, I was ten."

"When you were twenty-six, I was twenty-two." Evan nudged her arm with his elbow. "I'm gaining on you, huh?"

Lorna jumped up and grabbed the women's ten-speed by the handlebars. "I thought we came here to ride bikes, not talk about age-related things."

Evan stood, too. "You're right, so you lead—I'll follow."

They rode in pleasant silence, Lorna leading and Evan bringing up the rear. They were nearly halfway around the park when he pedaled alongside her. "You hungry? I brought along a few apples and some brownies I made last night."

She pulled her bicycle to a stop. "That does sound good. I haven't ridden a bike in years, and I'm really out of shape. A little rest and some nourishment might help get me going again."

Evan led them to a picnic table, set his kickstand, and

motioned her to take a seat. When they were both seated, he reached into his backpack and withdrew two Red Delicious apples, then handed one to Lorna. "Let's eat these first and save the brownies for dessert."

"Thanks." Lorna bit into hers, and a trickle of sweet, sticky juice dribbled down her chin. "Mmm. . .this does hit the spot." She looked over at him and smiled. "Sorry about being such a grump earlier. Guess I'm a little touchy about my age."

"Apology accepted. Uh. . .would you like to go to dinner when we're done riding?" Evan asked hesitantly.

Warning bells went off in Lorna's head, and she felt her whole body tremble. "I'm not dressed for going out."

"I was thinking about pizza. We don't have to be dressed up for that." Evan bit into his apple and grinned.

That dopey little smile and the gentleness in his eyes made Lorna's heartbeat quicken. She gulped. "I—I—"

"You can think about it while we finish our ride," Evan said, coming to her rescue.

She shrugged her shoulders. "Okay."

"So, tell me about Lorna Patterson."

"What do you want to know?"

"I know you're enrolled in a Christian college. Does that mean you're a believer in Christ?"

She nodded. "I accepted the Lord as my personal Savior when I was ten years old. At that time I thought I knew exactly what He wanted me to do with my life."

"Which was?"

"To teach music. I started playing piano right around

the time I became a Christian, and I soon discovered that I loved it."

"You're definitely a gifted pianist," he said with a broad smile. "You do great accompanying our choir, and you have a beautiful singing voice."

"Thanks." She nodded at him. "Is that all you wanted to know about me?"

"Actually, there is something else I've been wondering about."

"What?"

"You mentioned that you're a widow. How did your husband die?"

Lorna stared off into the distance, focusing on a cluster of pigeons eating dry bread crumbs someone had dumped on the grass. She didn't want to talk about Ron, her loss, or how he'd been killed so tragically.

"If you'd rather not discuss it, that's okay." Evan touched her arm gently. "I probably shouldn't have asked, but I want to know you better, so—"

Lorna turned her head so she was looking directly at him. "It's okay. It'll probably do me more good to talk about it than it will to keep it bottled up." She drew in a deep breath and plunged ahead. "Ron was killed in a motorcycle accident a little over a year ago. A semitruck hit him."

"I'm so sorry. It must have been hard for you."

"It was. Still is, in fact."

"Have you been on your own ever since?"

She shook her head. "Not exactly. I've been living with

Ron's parents, hoping it would help the three of us deal with our grief."

"And has it?"

"Some."

Compassion showed in Evan's eyes, and he took hold of her hand. It felt warm and comforting, and even though Lorna's head told her to pull away, her heart said something entirely different. So she sat there, staring down at their intertwined fingers and basking in the moment of comfort and pleasure.

"I'm surprised a woman your age, who's blessed with lots of talent and good looks, hasn't found another man by now."

Lorna felt her face flame. She focused on the apple core in her other hand, already turning brown. When she spotted a garbage can a few feet away, Lorna stood up. Before she could take a step, she felt Evan's hand on her arm.

"I'm sorry, Lorna. I can tell I've upset you. Was it my question about your husband's death, or was it the fact that I said I was surprised you hadn't found another man?"

She blinked away unwanted tears. "A little of both, I suppose."

She stiffened as Evan's arm went around her shoulders. "Still friends?"

"Sure," she mumbled.

"Does that mean you'll have pizza with me?"

"I thought I had until the bike ride was over to decide."

He twitched his eyebrows. "What can I say? I'm not the patient type."

"No, but you're certainly persistent."

He handed her a napkin and two brownies. "How do you think I've gotten this far in life?"

She sucked in her breath. How far had he gotten? Other than the fact that he was majoring in psychology, wasn't married, and was four years younger than she, Lorna knew practically nothing about Evan Bailey. Maybe she should learn more—in case she needed another friend.

She tossed the apple core into the garbage and bit into one of the brownies. "Where'd you say you got these?"

"Made them myself. I think I already told you that I'm taking an online cooking class. Right now the instructor is teaching us how to make some tasty sweet treats." He winked at her. "I thought it might make me a better catch if I could cook."

Lorna wasn't sure what to say. She didn't want to hurt Evan's feelings by telling him the brownie was too dry. She thought about the cookies he'd given her the other day. She'd tried one at lunch, and they had been equally dry, not to mention a bit overdone. Apparently the man was so new at cooking, he couldn't tell that much himself. She ate the brownie in silence and washed it down with the bottled water Evan had also supplied. When she was done, Lorna climbed onto her bike. "We'd better go. I hear the best pizza in town is at Mama Mia's!"

CHAPTER 6

Lorna slid into a booth at the pizza parlor, and Evan took the bench across from her. When their waitress came, they ordered a large combination pizza and a pitcher of iced tea.

As soon as the server was gone, Evan leaned forward on his elbows and gave Lorna a crooked smile. "You're beautiful, you know that?"

She gulped. No one but Ron had ever looked at her as if she were the most desirable woman on earth. Lorna leaned back in her seat and slid her tongue across her bottom lip. "Now it's your turn to tell me about Evan Bailey," she said, hoping the change in subject might calm her racing heart and get her thinking straight again.

She watched the flame flicker from the candle in the center of the table and saw its reflection in Evan's blue eyes. "My life

is an open book, so what would you like to know?" he asked.

I'd like to know why you're looking at me like that. "You told our group in class that your major is psychology, but you never said what you plan to do with it once you graduate," she said, instead of voicing her thoughts.

The waitress brought two glasses and a pitcher of iced tea to the table. As soon as she left, Evan poured them both a glass. "I'm hoping to land a job as a school guidance counselor, but if that doesn't work out, I might go into private practice as a child psychologist."

Lorna peered at him over the top of her glass. "Let me guess. I'll bet you plan to analyze kids all day and then come home at night to the little woman who's been busy taking care of your own children. Is that right?"

He chuckled. "Something like that."

"How come you're not married already and starting that family?"

He ran his fingers through his short-cropped, sandy-brown hair. "Haven't had time."

"No?"

"I was born and raised in Moscow, Idaho, and I'm the only boy in a family of three kids. I enrolled in Bible college shortly after I graduated high school, but I never finished."

"I take it you're a Christian, too?"

He nodded. "My conversion came when I was a teenager."

"How come you never finished Bible college?" she questioned.

"I decided on a tour of duty with the United States Air

Force instead." A muscle jerked in his cheek, and he frowned slightly. "I had a relationship with a woman go sour on me. After praying about it, I figured the best way to get over her was to enlist and get as far away from the state of Idaho as I could."

In the few weeks she'd known Evan, this was the first time Lorna had seen him look so serious, and it took her completely by surprise. She was trying to decide how to comment, when the waitress showed up with their pizza. Lorna was almost relieved at the interruption. At least now she could concentrate on filling her stomach and not her mind.

After a brief prayer, Evan began attacking his pizza with a vengeance. It made Lorna wonder when his last good meal had been. By the time she'd finished two pieces, Evan had polished off four slices and was working on another one. He glanced at Lorna's plate. "Aren't you hungry?"

"The pizza is great. I'm enjoying every bite," she said.

He swiped the napkin across his face and stared at Lorna. It made her squirm.

"Why are you looking at me that way?"

"What way?"

"Like I've got something on my face."

He chuckled. "Your face is spotless. I was thinking how much I enjoy your company and wondering if we might have a future together."

Lorna nearly choked on the piece of pizza she'd just put in her mouth. "Well, I—uh—don't think we're very well suited, and isn't it a little soon to be talking about a future together?"

"I'm not ready to propose marriage, if that's what you're thinking." His eyes narrowed. "And please don't tell me you're hung up about our age difference." Evan looked at Lorna so intently she could feel her toes curl inside her tennis shoes.

"That doesn't bother me so much. We're only talking about four years."

"Right." Evan raised his eyebrows. "You couldn't be afraid of men, or you wouldn't have been married before."

"I am not afraid of men! Why do you do that, anyway?"

"Do what?"

"Try to goad me into an argument."

He chuckled behind another slice of pizza. "Is that what you think I'm doing?"

"Isn't it?"

He dropped the pizza to his plate, reached across the table, and took hold of her hand.

She shivered involuntarily and averted her gaze to the table. "I wish you wouldn't do that either."

"Do what? This?" He made little circles on her hand with his index finger.

She felt warmth travel up her neck and spread quickly to her cheeks. "The way you look at me, I almost feel—"

"Like you're a beautiful, desirable woman?" He leaned farther across the table. "You are, you know. And I don't care about you being four years older than me. In fact, I think dating an older woman might have some advantages."

She pulled her hand away. "And what would those be?"

He crossed his arms and leaned back in his seat. "Let's see

now. . . . You'd be more apt to see things from a mature point of view."

"And?"

"Just a minute. I'm thinking." Evan tapped the edge of his plate with his thumb. "Since you're older, you're most likely wiser."

She clicked her tongue. "Sorry I asked."

"Would you be willing to start dating me?" he asked with a hopeful expression.

She shook her head. "I'm flattered you would ask, but I don't think it's a good idea."

"Why not?"

Something indefinable passed between them, but Lorna pushed it aside. "I have my heart set on finishing college, and nothing is going to stop me this time."

He gave her a quizzical look. "This time?"

Lorna ended up telling him the story of how she'd sacrificed her own career and college degree to put her husband through school. She ended it by saying, "So, you see, for the first time in a long while, I'm finally getting what I want."

"That's it? End of story?"

She nodded. "It will be when I graduate and get a job teaching music at an elementary school."

"Why not teach at a junior or senior high?"

"I like children—especially those young enough to be molded and refined." She wrinkled her nose. "The older a child is, the harder to get through to his creativity."

"Does that mean I won't be able to get through to your

creative side?" he asked with a lopsided grin.

"Could be." She folded her napkin into a neat little square and lifted her chin. "I really need to get home. I've got a lot of homework to do, and I've wasted most of the day."

Evan's sudden scowl told her she'd obviously hurt his feelings. "I didn't mean *wasted*. It's just that—"

He held up his hand. "No explanations are necessary." He stood, pulled a few coins from his back pocket, and dropped them on the table. "I hope that's enough for a tip, 'cause it's all the change I have."

She fumbled in her jacket pocket. "Maybe I have some ones I could add."

"Please don't bother. This will be enough, and I sure don't expect you to pay for the tip."

"I don't mind helping out," she insisted.

"Thanks anyway, but I'll take care of it." With that, Evan turned and headed for the cash register.

Lorna stood there with her ears burning and her heart pounding so hard she could hear it echoing in her ears. The day had started off so well. What had gone wrong, and how had it happened?

Evan was already up front paying for the pizza, so Lorna dug into her pocket and pulled out a dollar bill, which she quickly dropped to the table. Maybe she'd made a mistake thinking she and Evan could be friends. He obviously wanted more, but she knew it was impossible. In fact, he was impossible. Impossible and poor.

Evan said good-bye to Lorna outside in the parking lot. He was almost glad they had separate cars and he wouldn't have to drive her home. He didn't understand how a day that had started out fun and carefree could have ended on such a sour note. From all indications, he'd thought Lorna was enjoying their time together, but when she said she'd wasted most of the day, he felt deflated, even though he hadn't admitted it to her. That, plus the fact that she seemed overly concerned about his not having enough tip money, had thrown cold water on their time together.

What had turned things around? Had it been the discussion about their age difference? Children? Or maybe it was the money thing. Lorna might think he'd been too cheap to leave a decent tip. That could be why she'd climbed into her little red car with barely a wave and said nothing about hoping to see him again. Of course, he hadn't made the first move on that account either.

"I thought she might be the one, Lord," Evan mumbled as he opened the door to his Jeep. Remembering the look on Lorna's face when she'd eaten the treat he'd given her earlier that day, he added, "Maybe I should have followed the recipe closer and added some chocolate chips to the top of those brownies."

CHAPTER 7

The following Monday morning in Anatomy, Evan acted as though nothing were wrong. In fact, he surprised Lorna by presenting her with a wedge of apple pie he said he'd made the night before.

"It's a little mushy, and the crust's kind of tough," he admitted, "but I sampled a slice at breakfast, and it seemed sweet enough, at least."

Lorna smiled politely and took the plastic container with the pie in it. It was nice of Evan to think of her, but if he thought the dessert would give him an edge, he was mistaken. Lorna was fighting her attraction to Evan, and to lead him on would sooner or later cause one or both of them to get hurt.

Probably me, she thought. *I'm usually the one who makes all the sacrifices, then loses in the end.* What good had come out of her putting Ron through college and med school? He'd been killed in a senseless accident, leaving Lorna with a broken heart, a mound of bills, and no career for herself. It was going to be different from now on though. She finally had her life back on track.

"You look kind of down in the mouth this morning," Evan said, nudging her arm gently with his hand. "Everything okay?"

She shrugged. "I'm just tired. I stayed up late last night trying to get all my homework done."

He pursed his lips. "Guess that's my fault. If you hadn't wasted your Saturday bike riding and having pizza with me, you'd have had lots more time to work on your assignments."

So Evan had been hurt by her comment about wasted time on Saturday. Lorna could see by the look in the man's eyes that his pride was wounded. She felt a sense of guilt sweep over her like a cascading waterfall. She hadn't meant to hurt him. As a Christian, Lorna tried not to offend anyone, although she probably had fallen short many times since Ron's death.

"Evan," she began sincerely, "I apologize for my offhanded remark the other day. I had a good time with you, and my day wasn't wasted."

He grinned at her. "Really?"

She nodded.

"Would you be willing to go out with me again—as friends?"

Lorna chewed on her lower lip as she contemplated his offer. "Well, maybe," she finally conceded.

"That's great! How about this Saturday night, if you've got the evening off from working at Farmen's."

"I only work on weeknights," she said.

"Good, then we can go bowling, out to dinner, to the movies. . .or all three."

She chuckled softly. "I think one of those would be sufficient, don't you?"

"Yeah, I suppose so. Which one's your choice?"

"Why don't you surprise me on Saturday night?"

"Okay, I will." Evan snapped his fingers. "Say, I'll need your address so I can pick you up."

Lorna felt as though a glass of cold water had been dashed in her face. There was no way she could allow Evan to come by her in-laws' and pick her up for what she was sure they would assume was a date. She couldn't hurt Ann and Ed that way. It wouldn't be fair to Ron's memory. Maybe she should have told Evan she was busy on Saturday night. Maybe. . .

"You gonna give me your address or not?"

Lorna blinked. "Uh—how about we meet somewhere, like we did last Saturday?"

His forehead wrinkled. "Are you ashamed for your folks to meet me?"

"I live with my in-laws, remember?"

"So?"

"They might not understand about my going out with you," she explained. "They're still not over the loss of their son."

Evan stared at her for several seconds but finally shrugged his shoulders. "Okay. If that's how you want it, we can meet at

Ivar's along the waterfront. I've been wanting to try out their famous fish and chips ever since I came to Seattle."

Lorna licked her lips. "That does sound good."

Evan opened his mouth to say something more, but their professor walked into the room. "We'll talk later," he whispered.

She nodded in response.

Lorna entered the choir room a few minutes early, hoping to get her music organized before class began. She noticed Evan standing by the bulletin board across the room. She hated to admit it, but he was fun to be around. Could he be growing on her?

When she took a seat at the piano and peeked over the stack of music, she saw Vanessa Brown step up beside Evan. "Are the names posted for the choir solos yet?" the vivacious redhead asked. "I sure hope I got the female lead." She looked up at Evan and batted her lashes. "Maybe you'll get the male lead, and then we can practice together. Our voices would blend beautifully, don't you think?"

Oh please, Lorna groaned inwardly. The omelet she'd eaten for breakfast that morning had suddenly turned into a lump in the pit of her stomach. She didn't like the sly little grin Evan was wearing, either. He was up to something, and it probably meant someone was in for a double dose of his teasing.

Evan stepped in front of Vanessa, blocking her view of the board. She let out a grunt and tugged on his shirtsleeve. "I can't see. What's it say?"

Evan held his position, mumbling something Lorna couldn't quite understand.

"Well?" Vanessa shouted. "Are you going to tell me what it says or not?"

He scratched the back of his head. "Hmm. . ."

"What is it? Let me see!"

Evan glanced over at Lorna, but she quickly averted her gaze, pretending to be absorbed in her music.

When she lifted her head, Lorna saw Vanessa slide under Evan's arm, until she was facing the bulletin board. She studied it for several seconds, but then her hands dropped to her hips and she whirled around. "That just figures!" She marched across the room and stopped in front of the piano, shooting Lorna a look that could have stopped traffic on the busy Seattle freeway. "I hope you're satisfied!"

Lorna was bewildered. "What are you talking about?"

"Professor Burrows chose *you* for the female solo!" Vanessa scowled at Lorna. "Just because you're older than the rest of us and play the piano fairly well shouldn't mean you get special privileges."

Lorna creased her forehead so hard she felt wrinkles form. "Why would you say such a thing?"

"The professor doesn't think you can do any wrong. She's always telling the class how mature you are and how you're the only one who ever follows directions."

Lorna opened her mouth to offer some kind of rebuttal, but before she got a word out, Evan's deep voice cut her off. "Now wait a minute, Vanessa. Lorna got the lead part for only one reason."

Vanessa turned to face Evan, who stood at her side in front of the piano. "And that would be?"

"This talented woman can not only play the piano, but she can sing. Beautifully, I might add." He cast Lorna a sidelong glance, and she felt the heat of a blush warm her cheeks.

Vanessa's dark eyes narrowed. "Are you saying *I* can't sing?"

"I don't think that's what he meant," Lorna interjected.

Vanessa slapped her hand on the piano keys with such force that Lorna worried the Baldwin might never be the same. "Let the man speak for himself!" She whirled around to face Evan. "Or does the cute little blond have you so wrapped around her finger that you can't even think straight? It's obvious you're smitten with her."

Evan opened his mouth as if he was going to say something, but Vanessa cut him off. "Don't try to deny it, Evan Bailey! I've seen the way you and Lorna look at each other." She sniffed deeply. "Is she trying to rob from the cradle, or are you looking for a mother figure?"

Evan's face had turned crimson. "I think this discussion is over," he said firmly.

"That's right—let's drop it," Lorna agreed.

Vanessa glared at Evan. "Be a good boy now, and do what Mama Lorna says."

He drew in a deep breath. "I'm warning you, Vanessa. . ."

"What are you going to do? Tell the teacher on me?" she taunted.

Lorna cleared her throat a couple of times, and both Evan and Vanessa turned to look at her. "We're all adults here, and

if getting the lead part means so much to you, I'll speak to the professor about it, Vanessa."

"I'll fight my own battles, thank you very much!" Vanessa squared her shoulders. "Unlike some people in this class, I don't need a mother to fix my boo-boos." She turned on her heels and marched out of the room.

Evan let out a low whistle. "What was that all about?"

Lorna shook her head slowly. "You don't know?"

He shrugged. "Not really. She said she wanted the solo part, you offered to give it to her, and she's still mad. Makes no sense to me." He snickered. "But then, I never was much good at understanding women. Even if I did grow up with two sisters."

Lorna pinched the bridge of her nose. How could the man be so blind? "Vanessa is jealous."

"I know. She wants your part," Evan said, dropping to the bench beside Lorna. "She can't stand the fact that someone has a better singing voice than she does."

"I think the real reason Vanessa's jealous is because she thinks you like me, and she's attracted to you."

Evan looked at Lorna as though she'd lost her mind. "I've done nothing to make Vanessa think she and I might—"

"That doesn't matter. You make people laugh, and your manner is often flirtatious."

Evan rubbed his chin and frowned. "What can I say? I'm a friendly guy, but that doesn't mean I'm after every woman I meet."

Lorna reached for a piece of music. "Tell that to Vanessa Brown."

CHAPTER 3

Evan moved away from the piano, wishing there were something he could say or do to make Lorna feel more comfortable about the part she'd gotten. The scene with Vanessa had been unreal, but the fact that Lorna was willing to give up the solo part she'd been offered was one more proof that she lived her Christianity and would make a good wife for some lucky man. It just probably wasn't him.

He took a seat in the chair he'd been assigned and studied Lorna. She was thumbing through a stack of music, her forehead wrinkled and her face looking pinched. Was she still thinking about the encounter with Vanessa, frustrated with Evan, or merely trying to concentrate on getting ready for their first choir number?

Not only was Lorna a beautiful, talented musician, but she

had a sensitivity that drew Evan to her like a powerful magnet. Anyone willing to give up a favored part and not get riled when Vanessa attacked her with a vengeance made a hit with Evan. Lorna had done the Christian thing, even if Vanessa hadn't. Now if he could only convince her to give their relationship a chance. Maybe their Saturday night date would turn the tide.

Lorna had just slipped on her Farmen's apron when Chris came up behind her. "How was school today?"

"Don't ask."

"That bad, huh?"

"Afraid so."

"You've been back in college for a couple of weeks. I thought you'd be getting used to the routine by now."

Lorna grabbed an order pad from the back of the counter and stuffed it in her apron pocket. "The routine's not the problem."

Chris's forehead wrinkled. "What is, then?"

Lorna rubbed the back of her neck, trying to get the kinks out. "Never mind. It's probably not worth mentioning."

"It doesn't have anything to do with Evan Bailey, does it?"

"No! Yes. Well, partially."

Chris glanced at the clock on the wall above the serving counter. "We've still got a few minutes until our shift starts. Let's go to the ladies' room, and you can tell me about it."

Lorna shook her head. "What's the point? Talking won't change anything."

Chris grabbed her arm and gave it a gentle tug. "Come on, friend. I know you'll feel better once you've opened up and told me what's bothering you."

"Oh, all right," Lorna mumbled. "Let's hurry though. I don't want to get docked any pay for starting late."

Lorna was glad to discover an empty ladies' room when she and Chris arrived a few moments later. Chris dropped onto the small leather couch and motioned Lorna to do the same. "Okay, spill it!"

Lorna curled up in one corner of the couch and let the whole story out, beginning with her entering the choir room that morning and ending with Vanessa's juvenile tantrum and Evan's response to it all.

Chris folded her hands across her stomach and laughed. It wasn't some weak, polite little giggle, like Lorna offered her customers. It was a genuine, full-blown belly laugh.

Lorna didn't see what was so funny. In fact, retelling the story had only upset her further. "This is no laughing matter, Chris. It's serious business."

Her friend blinked a couple of times and then burst into another round of laughter.

Lorna started to get up. "Okay, fine! I shouldn't have said anything to you—that's obvious."

Chris reached over and grabbed hold of Lorna's arm. "No, stay, please." She wiped her eyes with the back of her hand. "I hope you know I wasn't laughing at you."

"Who?"

"The whole scenario." Chris clicked her tongue. "I just

don't get you, Lorna."

"What do you mean?"

"Evan Bailey is one cute guy, right?"

Lorna nodded and flopped back onto the couch.

"From what you've told me, I'd say the man has high moral standards and is lots of fun to be with."

"Yes."

Chris leaned toward Lorna. "If you don't wake up and hear the music, you might lose the terrific guy to this Vanessa person. If I'd been you today, I don't think I could have been so nice about things." She grimaced. "Offering to give up the part—now that's Christianity in action!"

Lorna crossed her legs and swung her foot back and forth, thinking the whole while how tempted she had been to give that feisty redhead a swift kick this afternoon. She'd said what she felt was right at the time, but it hadn't been easy.

"From all you've told me, I'd say it's pretty obvious the woman has her sights set on Evan Bailey." Chris shook her finger at Lorna. "You need to put this whole age thing out of your mind and give the guy a chance."

Lorna cringed. "That's not really the problem. I think Evan is as poor as a church mouse."

"What gives you that idea?"

Lorna quickly related the story of her and Evan's bicycle ride and how when they'd had pizza, he didn't have enough money to leave a decent tip.

Chris groaned. "Don't you think you're jumping to conclusions? Maybe the guy just didn't have much cash on him that day." She squinted her eyes. "And even if he is dirt poor, does it really matter so much?"

"It does to me. I don't want to get involved with another man who will expect me to give up my career and put him through college."

Evan was excited about his date with Lorna tonight. He'd been looking forward to it all week and had even tried his hand at making another online sweet treat, which he planned to give Lorna after dinner this evening. It was called Lemon Supreme and consisted of cream cheese mixed with lemon juice, sugar, eggs, and vanilla. Graham cracker crumbs were used for the crust, and confectioner's sugar was sprinkled over the top. He hadn't had time to sample it, but Evan was sure Lorna would like it.

At six o'clock sharp, Evan stood in front of Ivar's Restaurant along the Seattle waterfront. He was pleased when he saw Lorna cross the street and head in his direction. He'd been worried she might stand him up.

"Am I late?" she panted. "I had a hard time finding a place to park."

"You're right on time," he assured her. "I got here a few minutes ago and put my name on the waiting list at the restaurant."

"How long did they say we might have to wait for a table?"

"Not more than a half hour or so," he said.

"Guess we could go inside and wait in the lobby."

Evan nodded. "Or we could stay out here awhile and enjoy the night air." He drew in a deep breath. "Ah, sure does smell fresh down by the water, doesn't it?"

She wrinkled her nose. "Guess that all depends on what you call fresh."

"Salt sea air and fish a-frying. . .now that's what I call fresh," he countered with a wide smile.

She poked him playfully on the arm. "You would say something like that."

He chuckled. "Ah, you know me so well."

"No, actually, I don't," she said with a slight frown.

"Then we need to remedy that." Evan gazed deeply into her eyes. "I'd sure like to know you better,'cause what I've seen so far I really like."

Lorna gulped. Things were moving too fast, and she seemed powerless to stop them. What had happened to her resolve not to get involved with another man, or even to date? She had to put a stop to this before it escalated into more than friendship.

Before she had a chance to open her mouth, Evan took hold of her hand and led her to a bench along the side of the building. It faced the water, where several docks were located. "Let's sit awhile and watch the boats come and go," he suggested.

"What about our dinner reservations?"

"They said they'd call my name over the loudspeaker when our table's ready. Fortunately, there's a speaker outside, too." Evan sat down, and Lorna did the same.

The ferry coming from Bremerton docked, and Lorna watched the people disembark. She hadn't been to Bremerton in a long time. She hardly went anywhere but work, school, church, and shopping once in a while. What had happened to the carefree days of vacations, fun evenings out, and days off? *Guess I gave those things up when I began working so Ron could go to school.* Working two jobs left little time for fun or recreation, and now that Lorna was in school and still employed at one job, things weren't much better. *I do have the weekends free,* her conscience reminded. *Maybe I deserve to have a little fun now and then.*

"You look like you're a hundred miles away," Evan said, breaking into her thoughts.

She turned her head and looked at him. "I was watching the ferry."

He lifted her chin with his hand. "And I've been watching you."

Before Lorna could respond, he tipped his head and brushed a gentle kiss against her lips. As the kiss deepened, she instinctively wrapped her arms around his neck.

"Bailey, party of two. . .your table is ready!"

Lorna jerked away from Evan at the sound of his name being called over the loudspeaker. "We—we'd better get in there," she said breathlessly.

"Right." Evan stood up, pulling Lorna gently to her feet.

She went silently by his side into the restaurant, berating herself for allowing that kiss. *I'll be on my guard the rest of the evening. No more dreamy looks and no more kisses!*

CHAPTER 9

Farmen's Restaurant was more crowded than usual on Monday night, and Lorna's boss had just informed her that they were shorthanded. With God's help, she would get through her shift, although she was already tired. It had been a busy weekend, and she'd had to cram in time for homework.

Lorna thought about her date with Evan on Saturday, which hadn't ended until eleven o'clock because they'd taken a ride on one of the sightseeing boats after dinner. She'd thoroughly enjoyed the moonlight cruise around Puget Sound, and when Evan walked Lorna to her car, he'd presented her with another of his desserts. This one was called Lemon Supreme, and she had tried it after she got home that night.

Lorna puckered her lips as she remembered the sour taste caused by either too much lemon juice or not enough sugar. *I doubt Evan will ever be a master baker,* she mused.

She glanced at her reflection in the mirror over the serving counter, checking her uniform and hair one last time as she contemplated the way Evan had looked at her before they'd said good night. He'd wanted to kiss her again; she could tell by his look of longing. She had prevented it from happening by jumping quickly into her car and shutting the door.

"I only want to be his friend," Lorna muttered under her breath as she strolled into the dining room.

She got right to work and took the order of an elderly couple. Then she moved across the aisle to where another couple sat with their heads bent over the menus.

The woman was the first to look up, and Lorna's mouth dropped open.

"Fancy meeting you here," Vanessa Brown drawled.

Before Lorna could respond, Vanessa's companion looked up and announced, "Lorna works here."

Lorna's hand began to tremble, and she dropped the order pad. Evan Bailey was looking at her as though nothing was wrong. Maybe his having dinner with Vanessa was a normal occurrence. Maybe this wasn't their first date.

Forcing her thoughts to remain on the business at hand, Lorna bent down to retrieve the pad. When she stood up again, Vanessa was leaning across the table, fussing with Evan's shirt collar.

Lorna cleared her throat, and Vanessa glanced over at her. "What's good to eat in this place?"

"Tonight's special is meat loaf." Lorna kept her focus

on the order pad.

"Meat loaf sounds good to me," Evan said.

"You're such a simple, easy-to-please kind of guy," Vanessa fairly purred.

Lorna swallowed back the urge to scream. She probably shouldn't be having these unwarranted feelings of jealousy, for she had no claim on Evan. He'd obviously lied to her the other day, when he denied any interest in Vanessa. A guy didn't take a girl out to dinner if he didn't care something about her. *He took me to dinner on Saturday. Does that mean he cares about both me and Vanessa? Or could Evan Bailey be toying with our emotions?*

Lorna turned to face Vanessa, feeling as though the air between them was charged with electricity. "What would you like to order?"

"I'm careful about what I eat, so I think I'll have a chicken salad with low-cal ranch dressing." Vanessa looked over at her dinner partner and batted her eyelashes. "Men like their women to be fit and trim, right, Evan?"

He shrugged his shoulders. "I can't speak for other men, but to my way of thinking, it's what's in a woman's heart that really matters. Outward appearances can sometimes be deceiving."

He cast Lorna a grin, and she tapped her pencil against the order pad impatiently. "Will there be anything else?"

Evan opened his mouth. "Yes, actually—"

"Why don't you bring us a couple of sugar-free mocha-flavored coffees?" Vanessa interrupted. She gave Evan a syrupy smile. "I hope you like that flavor."

"Well, I—"

"Two mochas, a meat loaf special, and one chicken salad, coming right up!" Lorna turned on her heels and hurried away.

Evan watched Lorna's retreating form. Her shoulders were hunched, and her head was down. Obviously she wasn't at her best. He could tell she'd been trying to be polite when she took their orders, but from her tone of voice and those wrinkles he'd noticed on her forehead, he was certain she was irritated about something.

Probably wondering what I'm doing here with Vanessa. Wish she had stuck around longer so I could have explained. Maybe I should have gone after her.

"Evan, are you listening to me?"

Evan turned his head. "What were you saying, Vanessa?"

"I'm glad I ran into you tonight. I wanted to ask your opinion on something."

"What's that?"

Vanessa leaned her elbows on the table and intertwined her fingers. "All day I've been thinking about that solo part I should have had."

"You're coming to grips with it, I hope."

She frowned. "Actually, I've been wondering whether I should have taken Lorna up on her offer to give the part to me. What do you think, Evan? Should I ask her about it when she returns with our orders?"

Evan grunted. "I can't believe you'd really expect her to

give you that solo. Professor Burrows obviously feels Lorna's the best one for the part, or she wouldn't have assigned it to her."

Vanessa wrinkled her nose. "And I can't believe the way you always stick up for that little blond. She's too old and too prim and proper for you, Evan. Why don't you wake up?"

Evan reached for his glass of water and took a big gulp, hoping to regain his composure before he spoke again. When he set the glass down, he leaned forward and looked Vanessa right in the eye. "I'm not hung up on age differences, and as far as Lorna being prim and proper, you don't know what you're talking about."

Vanessa blinked and pulled back like she'd been stung by a bee. "You don't have to be so mean, Evan. I was only trying to make you see how much better—"

She was interrupted when Lorna appeared at the table with their orders. Evan was glad he could concentrate on eating his meat loaf instead of trying to change Vanessa's mind about a woman she barely knew.

As Lorna placed Evan's plate in front of him, she was greeted with another one of his phony smiles. They had to be phony. No man in his right mind would be out with one woman and flirting with another. For that matter, most men didn't bring their date to the workplace of the woman he'd dated only two nights before. *Dated and kissed,* she fumed.

Lorna excused herself to get their beverages, and a short

time later she returned with two mugs of mocha-flavored coffee. She looked at Evan sitting across from Vanessa, and an unexpected yearning stirred within her soul. Why couldn't she be the one he was having dinner with tonight? All this time Lorna had been telling herself that she and Evan could only be friends, so it didn't make sense to feel jealousy over seeing him with Vanessa Brown.

Maybe I don't know my own heart. Maybe. . .

"This isn't low-cal dressing. I asked for low-cal, remember?"

Vanessa's sharp words pulled Lorna's disconcerting thoughts aside. "I think it is," she replied. "I turned in an order for low-cal dressing, and I'm sure—"

"I just tasted it. It's not low-cal!"

Lorna drew in a deep breath and offered up a quick prayer for patience. "I'll go check with the cook who filled your order."

She started to turn, but Vanessa shouted, "I want another salad! This one is drenched in fattening ranch dressing, and it's ruined."

Lorna was so aggravated her ears were ringing, yet she knew in order to keep her job at Farmen's she would need to be polite to all customers—even someone as demanding as Vanessa. "I'll be back with another salad."

As she was turning in the order for the salad, Lorna met up with her friend Chris.

"You don't look like the picture of happiness tonight," Chris noted. "What's the problem—too many customers?"

Lorna gritted her teeth. "Just two too many."

"What's that supposed to mean?"

Lorna explained about Evan and Vanessa being on a date and how Vanessa was demanding a new salad.

Chris squinted her eyes. "I thought you and Evan went to Ivar's on Saturday."

"We did."

"Then what's up with him bringing another woman here on a date?"

Lorna leaned against the edge of the serving counter and groaned. "He's two-faced. What can I say?"

"Want me to finish up with that table for you?"

Lorna sighed with relief. "Would you? I don't think I can face Evan and his date again tonight."

Chris patted Lorna's arm. "Sure. What are friends for?"

Lorna peered into the darkening sky, watching out the window as Evan and Vanessa left the restaurant. She thought it was strange when she saw them each get into their own cars, but she shrugged it off, remembering that she and Evan had taken separate vehicles on Saturday night. Maybe Evan didn't have time to pick Vanessa up for their date. Maybe she'd been out running errands. It didn't matter. Lorna's shift would be over in a few hours, and then she could go home, indulge in a long, hot bath, and crash on the couch in front of the fireplace. Maybe a cup of hot chocolate and some of Ann's famous oatmeal cookies would help soothe her frazzled nerves. Some pleasant music and a good inspirational novel to read could have her feeling better in no time.

Lorna moved away from the window and sought out her next customer. She had a job to do, and she wouldn't waste another minute thinking about Evan Bailey. If he desired someone as self-serving as Vanessa Brown, he could have her.

Determined to come up with a way to win Lorna's heart, Evan had decided to try another recipe from his online cooking class. This one was called Bodacious Banana Bread, and it looked fairly simple to make. Between the loaf of bread and the explanation he planned to give Lorna tomorrow at school, Evan hoped he could let her know how much he cared.

Whistling to the tune of "Jesus Loves Me," Evan set out the ingredients he needed: butter, honey, eggs, flour, salt, soda, baking powder, and two ripe bananas. In short order he had everything mixed. He poured the batter into a glass baking dish and pulled it off the counter. Suddenly his hand bumped a bowl of freshly washed blueberries he planned to have with a dish of vanilla ice cream later on. The bowl toppled over, and half the blueberries tumbled into the bread pan, on top of the banana mixture.

"Oh no," Evan moaned. "Now I've done it." He tried to pick the blueberries out, but too many had already sunk to the bottom of the pan.

"Guess I could bake it as is and hope for the best." Evan grabbed a wooden spoon and gave the dough a couple of stirs to ensure that the berries were evenly distributed. He figured it couldn't turn out any worse than the other desserts he'd foiled

since he first began the cooking class. That Lemon Supreme he'd been dumb enough to give Lorna without first tasting had been one of the worst. He'd sampled a piece after their date on Saturday night and realized he'd messed up the recipe somehow, because it wasn't sweet enough.

Two hours later the bread was done and had cooled sufficiently. Evan decided to try a slice, determined not to give any to Lorna if it tasted funny.

To Evan's delight, the bread was wonderful. The blueberries had added a nice texture to the sweet dessert, and it was cooked to perfection. "I think I'll call this my Blueberry Surprise," he said with a chuckle. "Sure hope it impresses Lorna, because I'm not certain I have any words that will."

CHAPTER 10

$\mathcal{G}$oing back to school the following day—knowing she would have to face both Evan and Vanessa—was difficult for Lorna. She didn't know why it should be so hard. Evan had made no commitment to her, nor she to him.

When she arrived at school, Lorna was surprised to see Evan standing in the hall just outside their anatomy class. He spotted her, waved, and held up a paper sack. "I have something for you, and we need to talk." His voice sounded almost pleading, and that in itself Lorna found unsettling.

"There's nothing to talk about." Lorna started to walk away, hoping to avoid any confrontations and knowing if they did talk, her true feelings might give her away.

Evan reached out and grabbed hold of her arm. When she turned to face him, he lifted his free hand and wrapped

a tendril of her hair around his finger. He leaned slightly forward—so close she could feel his breath on her upturned face. If she didn't do something quickly, she was sure she was about to be kissed.

Evan moved his finger from her hair to her face, skimming down her cheek, then along her chin.

Lorna shivered with a mixture of anticipation and dread, knowing she should pull away. Just as Evan's lips sought hers, the floor began to move and the walls swayed back and forth in a surreal manner. Lorna had heard of bells going off and being so much in love that it hurt, but if this weird sensation had anything to do with the way she felt about Evan, she didn't want any part of loving the man.

Evan grasped Lorna's shoulders as the floor tilted, and she almost lost her balance. Knowing she needed his support in order to stay on her feet, Lorna leaned into him, gripping both of his arms. "What's happening?" she rasped.

"I believe we're in the middle of a bad earthquake." Evan's face seemed etched with concern. It was a stark contrast from his usual smiling expression.

Lorna's eyes widened with dread. She looked down and thought she was going to be sick. The floor was moving rhythmically up and down. It reminded her of a ship caught in a storm, about to be capsized with the crest of each angry wave.

"This is a bad one!" Evan exclaimed. "We need to get under a table or something."

She looked around helplessly; there were no tables in the

hall and none in the anatomy class either. The room only had opera-style seats. "Where?"

Evan pulled her closer. "A doorway! We should stand under a doorway."

The door to their classroom was only a few feet away, but it took great effort for them to maneuver themselves into position. Lorna's heart was thumping so hard she was sure Evan could hear each radical beat. She'd been in a few earthquakes during her lifetime, but none so violent as this one.

A candy machine in the hallway vibrated, pictures on the wall flew in every direction, and a terrible, cracking sound rent the air as the windows rattled and broke. A loud crash, followed by a shrill scream, sent shivers up Lorna's spine. There was no one else in the hallway, which was unusual, considering the fact that classes were scheduled to begin soon. Where was everybody, and when would this nightmare end?

Another ear-piercing sound! Was that a baby's cry? No, it couldn't be. This was Bay View Christian College, not a daycare center.

"I think the scream came from over there," Evan said, pointing across the hall. He glanced down at Lorna. "Did that sound like a baby's cry to you?"

She nodded and swallowed against the lump lodged in her throat.

"Stay here. I'll be right back." Evan handed Lorna the paper sack he'd been holding.

"No, don't leave me!" She clutched the front of his shirt as panic swept through her in a wave so cold and suffocating, she

thought she might faint.

"I think you'll be okay if you wait right here," he assured her. "Pray, Lorna. Pray."

The walls and floor were still moving, though a bit slower now. Lorna watched helplessly as Evan half crawled, half slid on his stomach across the hall. When he disappeared behind the door, she sent up a prayer. "Dear God, please keep him safe."

At that moment, the truth slammed into Lorna with a force stronger than any earthquake. Although she hadn't known Evan very long, she was falling in love with him. In the few short weeks since they'd met, he had brought joy and laughter into her life. He'd made her feel beautiful and special, something she hadn't felt since Ron's untimely death. They had a common bond. Both were Christians and interested in music, and each had a desire to work with children.

Children. The word stuck in Lorna's brain. She had always wanted a child. When she married Ron, Lorna was sure they would start a family as soon as he finished med school. That never happened because her husband had been snatched away as quickly as fog settles over Puget Sound.

She leaned heavily against the door frame and let this new revelation sink in. Was going back to school and getting her degree really Lorna's heart's desire? Or was being married to someone she loved and starting a family what she truly wanted? *It doesn't matter. I can't have a relationship with Evan because he doesn't love me. He's been seeing Vanessa.*

"Lorna! Can you come over here?" Evan's urgent plea

broke into her thoughts, and she reeled at the sound of his resonating voice.

The earthquake was over now, but Lorna knew from past experience that a series of smaller tremors would no doubt follow. She made her way carefully across the hall and into the room she'd seen Evan enter only moments ago.

She stopped short inside the door. In the middle of the room lay a young woman. A bookcase had fallen across her legs, pinning her to the floor. Lorna gasped as she realized the woman was holding a crying baby in her arms. The sight brought tears to Lorna's eyes. Covering her mouth to stifle a sob, she raced to Evan's side and dropped down beside him. She noticed beads of perspiration glistening on his upper lip. "Is she hurt badly? What about the baby?" Tears rolled down Lorna's cheeks as she thought about the possibility of a child losing its mother, or the other way around. *Please, God, let them be all right.*

"The woman's legs could be broken, so it wouldn't be good to try to move her. The baby appears to be okay." He pointed to the sobbing infant. "Could you pick her up, then go down the hall and find a phone? We need to call 911 right away."

Lorna nodded numbly. As soon as she lifted the child into her arms, the baby's crying abated. She stood and started for the door. Looking back over her shoulder, she whispered, "I love you, Evan, even if you do care for Vanessa Brown."

The next few hours went by in a blur. A trip to the hospital

in Evan's car, following the ambulance that transported the injured woman. . . Talking with the paramedics who'd found some identification on the baby's mother. Calling the woman's husband on the phone. Pacing the floor of the hospital waiting room. Trying to comfort a fussy child. Waiting patiently until the father arrived. Praying until no more words would come. Lorna did all these things with Evan by her side. They said little to each other as they waited to hear of the mother's condition. Words seemed unnecessary as Lorna acknowledged a shared sense of oneness with Evan, found only in a crisis situation.

The woman, who'd been identified as Sherry Holmes, had been at the college that morning looking for her husband, an English professor. He'd left for work without his briefcase, and she'd come to deliver the papers he needed. Professor Holmes wasn't in his class when she arrived. He'd been to an early morning meeting in another building, as had most of the other teachers. Why there weren't any other students in the hallway, Lorna still did not understand. She thought it must have been divine intervention, since so much structural damage had been done to that particular building. Who knew how many more injuries might have occurred had there been numerous students milling about?

Lorna felt a sense of loss as she handed the baby over to her father a short time later. She was relieved to hear that the child's mother was in stable condition, despite a broken leg and several bad bruises.

"You look done in," Evan said, taking Lorna's hand and leading her to a chair. He pointed to the paper sack lying on the table in the waiting room, where Lorna had placed it when they first arrived. "You never did open your present."

She nodded and offered him a weak smile. "Guess I've been too busy with other things." She pulled it open and peeked inside. A sweet banana aroma overtook her senses, and she sniffed deeply. "I'm guessing it's a loaf of banana bread."

Evan smiled. "It started out to be, but in the end, it turned out to be a kind of blueberry surprise."

She tipped her head and squinted her eyes. "What?"

Evan chuckled. "It's a long story." He motioned to the sack. "Try a hunk. I think you'll be pleasantly surprised."

Lorna opened the bag and withdrew a piece of the bread. She took a tentative bite, remembering the other treats he'd given her that hadn't turned out so well. To her surprise, the blueberry-banana bread was actually good. It was wonderful, in fact. She grinned at him. "This is great. You should patent the recipe."

He smiled and reached for her hand. "I don't know what surprises me the most. . .the accidental making of a great-tasting bread or your willingness to be here with me now."

"It's been a pretty rough morning, and I'm thankful the baby and her mother are going to be okay," she said, making no reference to her willingness to be with Evan.

"The look of gratitude on Professor Holmes's face will stay with me a long time." Evan gazed deeply into Lorna's eyes. "Nothing is as precious as the life God gives each of us, and I don't want to waste a single moment of the time I have left on this earth." He stroked the side of her face tenderly. "You're the

most precious gift He's ever offered me."

Lorna blinked back sudden tears. "Me? But I thought you and Vanessa—"

Evan shook his head and leaned over to kiss her. When he pulled away, he smiled. Not his usual silly grin, but an honest "I love you" kind of smile. "I came to the restaurant last night to talk to you," he said. "I was going to plead my case and beg you to give our relationship a try."

"But Vanessa—"

"She was not my date."

"She wasn't?"

He shook his head.

"You were both at the same table, and I thought—"

"I know what you thought." He wrapped his arms around Lorna and held her tightly. "She came into Farmen's on her own, saw me sitting at that table, and decided to join me. The rest you pretty well know."

She shook her head. "Not really. From the way you two were acting, I thought you were on a date."

Evan grimaced. "Vanessa Brown is a spoiled, self-centered young woman." He touched the tip of Lorna's nose and chuckled. "Besides, she's too young for someone as mature as me."

Lorna laughed and tilted her head so she was looking Evan right in the eye. "In this life we don't always get second chances, but I'm asking for one now, Evan Bailey."

He smiled. "You've got it."

"I think it's time for you to meet my in-laws."

"I'd like that."

"And I don't care how poor you are either," she added, giving his hand a squeeze.

"What makes you think I'm poor?"

"You mean you're not?"

He shook his head. "Not filthy rich, but sure no pauper." He bent his head down to capture her lips in a kiss that evaporated any lingering doubts.

Lorna thought about the verse of scripture Ann had quoted her awhile back. *Take delight in the Lord, and he will give you the desires of your heart.* Her senses reeled with the knowledge that regardless of whether she ever taught music or not, she had truly found her heart's desire in this man with the blueberry surprise.

RECIPE FOR BLUEBERRY SURPRISE

⅓ cup butter
⅔ cup honey
2 eggs
2 ripe bananas, mashed
1¼ cups all-purpose flour
2 teaspoons baking powder
½ teaspoon salt
¼ teaspoon baking soda
1 cup blueberries

Cream butter and honey until fluffy. Add eggs one at a time, beating well after each addition. Add bananas and mix well. Combine dry ingredients and add to creamed mixture, mixing thoroughly. Gently fold in blueberries. Pour into 9x5-inch loaf pan lined with waxed paper. Bake at 350 degrees for 50 to 60 minutes or until wooden toothpick comes out clean. Cool, remove from pan, and gently pull away waxed paper. (Makes 1 loaf.)

GRANDMA'S DOLL

DEDICATION

In loving memory of my Aunt Margaret,
who gave me her Bye-Lo baby doll many years ago.
Thank you for the special treasure I will someday
give to one of my granddaughters.

CHAPTER 1

Sheila Nickels shivered as a blast of chilly March air pushed against her body. She slipped the tarnished key into the lock and opened the door. This was Grandma's house—the place where Sheila had come throughout her childhood for holidays, special occasions, and everything in between. She'd felt warmth, love, and joy whenever she visited this Victorian home on the north side of Casper, Wyoming.

Sheila stepped into the dark entryway and felt for the light switch on the wall closest to the door. "At least the electricity hasn't been turned off yet," she murmured.

An eerie sense of aloneness settled over her as she moved to the living room. Everything looked so strange. Much of Grandma's furniture was missing, and the pieces left had been draped with white sheets, including the upright piano Sheila

103

and her cousins used to plunk on. Several cardboard boxes sat in one corner of the room, waiting to be hauled away. It was a dreary sight.

A sigh stuck in Sheila's throat, and she swallowed it down. She'd just come from visiting her grandmother at Mountain Springs Retirement Center on the other side of town. Grandma's one-bedroom apartment looked like a fishbowl compared to this grand home where Grandma and Grandpa Dunmore had lived for over fifty years. Grandpa passed away two years ago, but Grandma had continued to stay here until she finally decided taking care of the house was too much for her. She'd moved to the retirement center a few weeks ago.

Grandma's old house didn't look the same without the clutter of her antique furniture. It didn't sound the same without Grandma's cheerful voice calling from the kitchen, "Girls, come have some chocolate chip cookies and a glass of milk."

Sheila slipped off her coat and draped it across the arm of an overstuffed chair. She then placed her purse on the oak end table and turned toward the stairs. She was here at her grandmother's request and needed to follow through with what she'd set out to do.

As a feeling of nostalgia washed over her, Sheila climbed the steps leading to the second floor. Another flight of stairs took her to the attic, filled with so many wonderful treasures. A chain dangled from the light fixture overhead, and Sheila gave it a yank.

"Kimber, Lauren, Jessica, and I used to play here," she whispered into the dusty, unfinished room. She lowered herself

to the lid of an antique trunk and closed her eyes, allowing the memories of days gone by to wash over her.

"Look at me, Sheila. Aren't I beautiful?"

Sheila giggled as her cousin Lauren pranced in front of her wearing a pair of black patent leather heels that were much too big for her seven-year-old feet. Wrapped in a multicolored crocheted shawl with a crazy-looking green hat on her head, Lauren continued to swagger back and forth.

"You can play dress-up if you want to, but I'm gonna get the Bye-Lo baby and take her for a ride." Sheila scrambled over to the wicker carriage, where the bisque-headed doll was nestled beneath a tiny patchwork quilt. Grandma had told her she'd made the covering many years ago when she was a little girl.

Of all the treasures in her grandmother's attic, the Bye-Lo baby was Sheila's favorite. She could play with it for hours while her three girl cousins found other things to do.

Sheila leaned over and scooped the precious doll into her arms. "Bye-Lo, I wish you could be mine forever."

Sheila's eyes snapped open as she returned to the present. Since Grandma had already moved, her house would soon be put up for sale. She'd called Sheila at her home in Fresno, California, and invited her to choose something from the attic that was special to her. Sheila knew right away what that *something* would be—the Bye-Lo baby doll. Some might think it was silly, but when she was a child, Sheila had prayed she could own the doll someday, and her prayers were finally being answered. Now all she had to do was find her treasure.

Sheila scanned the perimeter of the attic. An old dresser sat near the trunk, and an intricately designed wooden container was a few feet away. Her gaze came to rest on the small wicker doll carriage, which Bye-Lo used to lie in. It was empty.

"How odd. The doll always sat in that baby carriage." She stood and lifted the lid of the trunk. "Maybe it's in here."

Near the bottom she found several pieces of clothing that had belonged to the doll. There was even a photograph of young Sheila holding her favorite attic treasure. The dolls she had owned as a child hadn't been nearly as special as Bye-Lo. The church her father had pastored then was small and didn't pay much. Sheila had learned early in life to accept secondhand items and be grateful, but she'd always wished for more.

She grabbed the picture and placed it in the pocket of her blue jeans, then slammed the trunk lid. "That doll has to be in this house someplace, and I'm not leaving until I find it!"

The telephone jingled, and Dwaine Woods picked it up on the second ring. "The Older the Better," he said into the receiver. "May I help you?"

"Is Bill Summers there?" a woman's gravelly voice questioned.

"Sorry, but Bill's not here. He sold his business to me a few months ago."

"Oh, I see. Well, this is Lydia Dunmore, and I did some business with The Older the Better Antique Shop when Bill owned it."

"Is there something I can help you with, Ms. Dunmore?" Dwaine asked.

"As a matter of fact, there is. I'd like to see about having my old piano appraised. I've recently moved and will need to sell it."

"Sure. No problem. When would you like to have the appraisal done?"

"How about this afternoon? One of my granddaughters is at the house right now, and she could let you in."

Dwaine reached for a notepad and pen. "If you'll give me the address, I'll run over there and take a look. Would you like me to call you with my estimate, or should I give it to your granddaughter?"

"Just give it to Sheila. She'll be coming back to the retirement center where I live to return my house key sometime before she leaves Casper."

Dwaine wrote down the particulars, and a few minutes later he hung up the phone. Lydia Dunmore's house was on the other side of town, but he could be there in ten minutes. He put the CLOSED sign in the store's front window, grabbed his jacket off the antique coat tree, and headed out the door. Things had been slow at The Older the Better this week, but it looked like business might be picking up.

With an exasperated groan, Sheila shut the lid on the cedar

chest—the last place she had searched for Grandma's old doll. For the past couple of hours, she'd looked through countless boxes and trunks, organizing each one as she went. Except for the room being much cleaner now, her trip to the attic had been fruitless. There was no doll to be found.

"Grandma would probably tell me to choose something else," Sheila muttered, "but nothing here matters to me except the Bye-Lo baby."

Once more, Sheila thought about her grandmother's recent move and consoled herself with the fact that if Grandma hadn't left this rambling old house, Sheila and her girl cousins wouldn't have been asked to choose something special from the attic. The boy cousins had been invited to check out the basement for an item they would like to have.

"Too bad I can't find what's special to me," she grumbled.

Maybe the doll had been removed from the attic and was in one of the boxes downstairs. Sheila decided it was worth the time to take a look. She yanked on the chain to turn off the light and headed for the stairs. If she didn't find Bye-Lo in the next hour or so, she planned to head back to the retirement center. Maybe Grandma could shed some light on the doll's disappearance.

Sheila entered the living room and was about to kneel in front of a cardboard box when the doorbell rang. "I wonder who that could be."

She went to the front door and looked through the peephole. A man stood on the porch—an attractive man with sandy-blond hair and brown eyes. Sheila didn't recognize

him, but then she hadn't lived in Casper for twelve years and didn't get back for visits very often. The man could be one of Grandma's neighbors for all she knew. He could even be a salesman, a Realtor, or. . .

The bell rang again, and Sheila jumped. Should she open the door? She sent up a quick prayer. *Protect me, Lord, if this man's a criminal.*

She slipped the security chain in place and opened the door the few inches it would go. "May I help you?"

"Hi, I'm Dwaine Woods from The Older the Better Antique Shop across town. I got a call to come here and take a look at an old piano."

Sheila's gaze darted to the living room. Grandma obviously had left the piano behind because there wasn't enough room in her apartment at the retirement center. How sad that Grandma felt forced to sell something she'd dearly loved for so many years.

"I have my business card right here if you'd like to see it," Dwaine said, as if sensing her reservations about opening the door. He reached into his jacket pocket, pulled out a leather wallet, and withdrew a card. "I bought the place from Bill Summers not long ago." He slipped it through the small opening, and Sheila clasped the card between her thumb and index finger. She studied it a few seconds and decided it looked legitimate.

"Who asked you to look at the piano?" she asked with hesitation.

"Lydia Dunmore. She called awhile ago and said she'd

like an estimate. Told me her granddaughter Sheila was here and would let me in." He shuffled his feet across the wooden planks on the porch. "I presume that would be you?"

Sheila opened her mouth to reply, but the sharp ringing of the telephone halted her words. "I'd better get that. Be right back." She shut the door before Dwaine had a chance to say anything more.

Not knowing how long he might be expected to wait, Dwaine flopped into the wicker chair near the door. He couldn't believe how nervous the young woman seemed. She acted like she didn't believe Lydia Dunmore had called and asked him to give an estimate on the piano.

She must not be from around here. Most everyone I know is pretty trusting. Dwaine hadn't been able to get a good look at her face through the small opening in the doorway, but he had seen her eyes. They were blue, like a cloudless sky, and they'd revealed obvious fear.

Sure hope she comes back soon and lets me in. Now that the sun's going down, it's getting cold out here. Dwaine stuffed his hands inside his jacket pockets while he tapped his foot impatiently. Finally, he heard the door creak open. A young woman with jet-black hair curling around her face in soft waves stared at him.

"Sorry for making you wait so long," she said. "That was my grandmother on the phone. She called to let me know you were coming to look at the piano."

Dwaine stood. "Does that mean I can come in?"

She nodded, and her cheeks turned pink as a sunset. "I'm Sheila Nickels."

Dwaine stuck out his hand and was relieved when she shook it. Maybe now that her grandmother had confirmed the reason for his visit, Sheila wouldn't be so wary.

"It's nice to meet you. I take it you're not from around here?"

She motioned him to follow as she led the way to the living room. "I grew up in Casper, but twelve years ago my folks moved to Fresno, California. My father's a minister and was offered a job at a church there. I was fourteen at the time."

"So you're a Christian, then?"

She smiled. "I have been since I was twelve and went to Bible camp. That's when I acknowledged my sins and accepted Christ as my personal Savior."

Dwaine grinned back at her. "I'm a Christian, too, and it's always nice to meet others who have put their faith in the Lord."

She nodded. "I agree."

"What brings you to this part of the country?" he asked.

Sheila motioned to the array of boxes stacked in one corner of the room. "Grandma recently moved to Mountain Springs Retirement Center, and she'll be putting this old house on the market soon."

"Which is why she wants to sell the piano?"

"Right. Grandma called me a few weeks ago and asked that I come here. She said she'd like me to choose an item from the attic—something I felt was special. Since she needed it done before the house sold, I decided to take a week's vacation and fly here before everything's been gone through." Sheila sucked in her lower lip. "She asked each of her granddaughters to come, and I'm the first to arrive."

"Have you found what you wanted yet?" he questioned.

She shook her head. "It's an old doll I'm looking for, but there was no sign of it in the attic."

Dwaine massaged the bridge of his nose. "Hmm. . .did you ask your grandmother about it? Maybe she moved the doll to some other part of the house."

Sheila pulled out the wooden piano bench and sat down. "I would have asked her when we were on the phone a few minutes ago, but I didn't want to leave you on the porch in the cold."

"If you'd like to call her back, you two can talk about the missing doll while I take a look at this old relic," he said, motioning to the piano. "I should have an estimate by the time you get off the phone."

"That sounds fine." Sheila turned and walked out of the room.

Dwaine moved over to uncover the piano and smiled. *She's sure cute. Guess I'll have to wait till she comes back to find out if she's married or not.*

CHAPTER 2

*S*heila returned to the living room ten minutes later, a feeling of defeat threatening to weigh her down. She'd come all the way to Casper for nothing.

She tossed aside the white sheet on the aging, olive green sofa and groaned. "I can't believe it!"

Dwaine sat on the piano bench, writing something on a notepad, but he looked up when she made her comment. "Bad news?"

She nodded, not trusting her voice and afraid she might break into tears if she related her conversation with Grandma.

Dwaine's forehead wrinkled. "What'd your grandmother say about the doll?"

"It's gone." She paused and drew in a deep breath. "Grandma said she sold it to you."

113

He shook his head. "I've never met Lydia Dunmore. The first contact I've had with her was today, when she asked me to appraise this." He motioned toward the piano with his elbow.

"She said she took the Bye-Lo doll to The Older the Better Antique Shop last fall and sold it."

"That may be, but I wasn't the owner back then. I bought the place from Bill Summers two months ago."

Sheila sniffed. "Guess I'd better talk to him then. Do you have his home phone number or address?"

Dwaine fingered the small dimple in the middle of his chin. That, along with his sandy-blond hair and dark brown eyes, made him the most attractive man Sheila had met in a long time. *Of course, looks aren't everything,* she reminded herself. *Kevin Carlson was good-looking, too, and he broke my heart.*

"Bill moved to Canada right after he sold the store. I'm sorry to tell you this, but he's in the early stages of Alzheimer's, so his daughter and son-in-law came to Casper and moved him up there to be near them."

Sheila tapped her fingernails along the edge of the couch. "Are you saying he probably wouldn't remember what became of my grandmother's doll, even if I could contact him?"

"Exactly. The poor man wouldn't have been able to handle the details of selling the store if his family hadn't taken over and done all the paperwork." Dwaine shook his head. "It's sad to see an older person forced to give everything up when some unexpected illness overtakes his body or mind."

Sheila nodded and swallowed around the lump in her throat, feeling sad for Bill Summers and thankful Grandma

was still fairly healthy. Then her thoughts went to the doll she would never have, and unable to control her emotions, she covered her face and let the tears flow.

Dwaine stayed on the piano bench a few seconds, unsure of what to say or do. He didn't want Sheila to misread his intentions if he offered comfort. He wrestled with his thoughts a moment longer and finally realized he couldn't remain seated and do nothing but watch her cry.

He hurried across the room and took a seat beside her on the couch. "Would you like me to call someone—your husband, grandmother, or some other relative?"

"I–I'm not married," she said with a sniffle. "And I don't want to bother Grandma. She's got enough problems of her own right now." Sheila lifted her head and looked at him through dark, heavy lashes. Her blue eyes were luminous behind the tears that filled them, and her chin trembled as she made a feeble attempt at smiling. "Sorry for blubbering like that. I don't know what came over me."

"I'm not married either, and I may not know a lot about women, but I do have a sister who can get pretty emotional at times, so I try to be understanding when someone's in tears."

When Sheila offered him another half smile, Dwaine fought the urge to wipe away the remaining moisture on her cheeks. He couldn't explain the reason this dark-haired beauty made him feel protective. He'd just met the woman, so it made no sense at all.

"I'd like to help you find that doll," Dwaine announced.

Her eyes brightened some. "How?"

"The first place I want to look is my antique shop. Even though I haven't seen any Bye-Lo dolls lying around, she could still be there hidden away in some drawer, a box, or a closet."

Sheila's dark eyebrows disappeared under her curly bangs. "You think so?"

"It's worth checking. At the very least we ought to find a receipt showing the doll was brought into the shop, and if it was sold again, there should be a receipt for that, too." Dwaine returned to the piano bench, where he retrieved the notepad. He ripped off the top page, moved back to the sofa, and handed the paper to Sheila. "Here's the estimate on the piano. If you want to give me the phone number of the place where you're staying, I'll call you if and when I locate the doll."

She frowned. "I was hoping, before I return Grandma's house key, that I might go over to your shop and see what you can find out."

"I haven't been all that busy today, so I guess we could head over there now and take a look."

"I'd appreciate that." Sheila reached into her jeans pocket and withdrew a picture. "This is me as a child, holding the Bye-Lo, in case you're wondering what the doll looks like."

He nodded. "Yep. About the same as the ones I've seen advertised in doll collectors' magazines."

"I'm only here on a week's vacation, which means I won't be in Casper long. So if we could go to your shop now, that would be great."

It was obvious that Sheila was desperate to find her grandmother's doll, and Dwaine didn't have the heart to tell her it could take days or even weeks to go through everything in his store. Bill Summers hadn't been much of an organizer, not to mention the fact that he'd become forgetful toward the end. Dwaine had already discovered this was the reason so many things seemed to be missing or were found in some obscure places. Of course, Dwaine couldn't say much about being disorganized. Tidiness was not his best trait either.

"If you have your own car, you can follow me over to the shop. If not, I'll be happy to give you a lift," he offered.

"That won't be necessary. My rental's parked in the driveway."

"Sounds good. Are you ready to head out then?"

She nodded and grabbed her jacket from the arm of an overstuffed chair, then reached for her purse on the end table.

"Oh, and by the way," he said, turning back to the piano and lifting the sheet off the top, "I found this while I was doing my appraisal. It looks old, and I figured it might be a family treasure." He handed her a black Bible with frayed edges and several pages ready to fall out.

Sheila smiled. "Thanks. This must belong to Grandma. I'll take it to her when I return the house key. She probably didn't realize she left it on top of the piano."

Dwaine felt a sense of relief. At least Sheila was smiling again.

Sheila had never been inside an antique store so full of

clutter, but she remembered Dwaine saying the previous owner's memory had been fading. The poor man probably had struggled with keeping the shop going and hadn't been able to clean or organize things. For all she knew, Dwaine might not be any better at putting the place in order. He did seem to be kind and caring though, if one could tell anything from first impressions.

Kind, caring, and cute, Sheila mused as she followed Dwaine to a long wooden counter in the center of the store. An antique cash register sat on one end, and a cordless phone was beside it. An odd contrast, to be sure.

"I'll start by looking through the receipt box," Dwaine said as he reached under the counter and retrieved a battered shoe box that looked like it belonged in the garbage.

Sheila stifled a groan. *That's where he keeps his receipts? I'd say this man's in need of a good secretary as well as some new office supplies.*

While Dwaine riffled through the papers, Sheila leaned against the front of the counter and reflected on her job back in Fresno. For the last two years, she'd worked as a receptionist in a chiropractor's office. The clinic had been in total disarray when she was hired, and it had taken nearly six months to get everything organized. She'd finally succeeded, and the office was running more smoothly and efficiently than ever before. Dr. Taylor often praised Sheila for her organizational skills.

"Do you miss living in Wyoming, or are you a bona fide California girl now?" Dwaine asked, breaking into Sheila's thoughts.

"I like my job working as a receptionist for a chiropractor," she replied, "but I miss some things about living here."

"Such as?"

"Grandma for one. I used to love going over to her house and playing in the attic with my girl cousins. There were so many wonderful treasures there." She wrinkled her nose. "The boy cousins preferred to play outside or in the basement where they could get dirty and look for creepy crawlers."

Dwaine chuckled. "Anything else you miss about living in Casper?"

"The cold, snowy winters, when we went sledding and ice-skating."

"Guess you don't get much snow in California, huh?"

"Not in Fresno."

Dwaine laid the stack of receipts he'd already gone through on the countertop. "Is Lydia Dunmore your only relative living here now?"

"My cousin Jessica is still in the area, and so is Aunt Marlene. Mom and Dad are missionaries in Brazil, my brother lives in San Diego, and the rest of my aunts, uncles, and cousins have moved to other parts of the country."

Dwaine scratched the side of his head. "Most of my family lives in Montana, and my sister lives in Seattle, Washington. We all keep in touch through phone calls and e-mail."

Sheila nodded and fought the urge to grab a handful of receipts and begin searching for anything that might help find her missing Bye-Lo baby. Her conversation with Dwaine was pleasant, but it wasn't accomplishing a lot.

A few minutes later, Dwaine laid the last piece of paper on top of the stack. "There's nothing here that would indicate a Bye-Lo doll was bought or sold last fall, and these receipts go clear back to the beginning of April that year."

Sheila resented his implication, and she bristled. "Are you suggesting my grandmother just *thought* she brought the doll here and sold it to Bill Summers?"

Dwaine's ears turned pink as he shoved the receipts back into the shoe box. "I'm not saying that at all. Since Bill was so forgetful, it's possible he either didn't write up a receipt or filed it someplace other than the shoe box."

Which is a dumb place to file anything. Sheila forced a smile. "Now what do we do?"

Dwaine patted his stomach. "I don't know about you, but I'm starving. How about we go to the café next door and get some grub? Then, if you have the time, we can come back here and check a few other places."

Sheila's stomach rumbled at the mention of food. She hadn't taken time for lunch this afternoon, and breakfast had consisted of only a cup of coffee and a bagel with cream cheese. A real meal might be just what she needed right now.

She slung her purse over her shoulder. "Dinner sounds good to me."

Dwaine lifted one eyebrow and tipped his head. "Around here it's called supper."

She grinned up at him. "Oh, right. How could I have forgotten something as important as that?"

CHAPTER 3

asper's Café wasn't the least bit crowded, but this was Wednesday, and Sheila remembered that most people didn't go out to eat in the middle of the week. At least not around these parts.

Sheila studied the menu place mat in front of her, although she didn't know why. She and Dwaine had already placed their orders for sirloin steaks and baked potatoes. It was more than she normally ate, but for some reason Sheila felt ravenous. Maybe it was the company. She felt comfortable sitting here in a cozy booth, inside a quaint restaurant, with a man who had the most gorgeous brown eyes she'd ever seen.

Dwaine smiled from across the table. "You remind me of someone."

"Who?"

He fingered the dimple in his chin. "I'm not sure. Shirley Temple, maybe."

Sheila squinted her eyes. "Shirley Temple had blond hair, and mine's black as midnight."

"True, but her hair was a mass of curls, and so is yours."

She reached up to touch the uncontrollable tendrils framing her face. Her hair had always been naturally curly, and when she was a child, she'd liked not having to do much with it. Now Sheila simply endured the nasty curls, envying others with straight, sleek hair.

He traced his fingers along the edge of the table. "Do you know what an original Shirley Temple doll is worth on today's market?"

She shook her head.

"Several hundred dollars."

"Wow. That's impressive."

"Your lost Bye-Lo baby's going for a tidy sum, too."

"Really?"

He nodded. "I saw an eighteen-inch Bye-Lo listed in a doll collectors' magazine several weeks ago, and it cost a thousand dollars."

Sheila's mouth fell open. "That's a lot of money. I had no idea the doll was so valuable."

"Actually, the eight-inch version, like your grandmother had, is only selling for five hundred dollars."

"Only?"

"You see that as a bad thing?"

"It is for me, since I don't have the doll or that kind

of money lying around."

"We're going to find it," Dwaine said with the voice of assurance, "and it might not cost as much as you think. If the doll's still at my shop, I can sell her back to you for whatever Bill Summers paid your grandmother, which I'm sure wasn't nearly as much as the doll is worth."

Sheila's heart hammered. Why should she be forced to buy something she was told she could have? Of course, Grandma hadn't actually said Sheila could have the doll. It had been sold several months ago, and Grandma probably figured there were lots of other things in the attic Sheila could pick from.

She squeezed her eyes shut, hoping to ward off the threatening tears. It might be childish, but she wanted that doll and nothing else.

"You okay?"

Sheila felt Dwaine's hand cover hers, and her eyes snapped open. "I–I'm fine. If you can find the doll, I'll pay you whatever you think it's worth."

"I'll do my best."

Sheila studied Dwaine's features—the prominent nose, velvet brown eyes, sandy-blond hair, and heavy dark eyebrows. He looked so sincere when he smiled. Hopefully he meant what he said about helping find the precious Bye-Lo baby. Maybe he wasn't like Kevin, who'd offered her nothing but lies and broken promises.

"You mentioned earlier that your folks are missionaries in Brazil."

"Yes. They've been living there for the past year."

"That sounds exciting. My church sent a work and witness team to Argentina last summer. The group said it was a worthwhile experience."

"Are you active in your church?" Sheila questioned.

He reached for his glass of water and grinned at her. "I teach a teen Sunday school class. Ever since I accepted the Lord as my Savior, I've wanted to work with young people." He chuckled. "I was only fourteen at the time of my conversion, so I had to grow up and become an adult before they'd let me teach."

Sheila relaxed against her seat. *Why couldn't I meet someone as nice as you in Fresno?* She shook her head, hoping to get herself thinking straight again. Her vacation would be over in a week, and then she'd be going back to California. It might be some time before she returned to Casper for another visit. Dwaine Woods could be married by then.

"So if your folks live in Brazil and your brother lives in San Diego, what's keeping you in Fresno?" Dwaine asked.

"My job, I guess." Sheila fingered her napkin. What was taking their order so long?

"That's all? Just a job?"

She nodded. "As I said earlier, I work as a receptionist at a chiropractor's office."

Dwaine leaned his elbows on the table and looked at her intently. "You're so pretty, I figure there must be a man in your life."

Sheila felt her face heat up. Was Dwaine flirting with her? He couldn't be; they barely knew each other. "There is no man

in my life." *Not anymore.*

She was relieved when their waitress showed up. The last thing she wanted to talk about was her broken engagement to Kevin. She was trying to put the past to rest.

"Sorry it took so long," the middle-aged woman said as she set plates in front of them. "We're short-handed in the kitchen tonight, and I'm doing double duty." There were dark circles under her eyes, and several strands of gray hair crept out of the bun she wore at the back of her neck.

"We didn't mind the wait," Dwaine said. He smiled at Sheila and winked. "It gave me a chance to get better acquainted with this beautiful young woman."

His comment made her cheeks feel warm, and she reached for her glass of water, hoping it might cool her down.

"Would you mind if I prayed before we eat?" he asked when the waitress walked away.

"Not at all." Sheila bowed her head as Dwaine's deep voice sought the Lord's blessing on their meal and beseeched God for His help in finding her grandmother's doll.

Maybe everything would work out all right after all.

Dwaine became more frustrated by the minute. They'd been back at his shop for more than an hour and had looked through every drawer and cubbyhole he could think of. There was no sign of any Bye-Lo doll or even a receipt to show there ever had been one.

"Maybe your grandmother took the doll to another

antique shop," he said to Sheila, who was searching through a manila envelope Dwaine had found in the bottom of his desk.

"She said she brought it here."

"Maybe she forgot."

Sheila sighed. "I suppose she could have. Grandma recently turned seventy-five, and her memory might be starting to fade."

Dwaine looked at the antique clock on the wall across the room and grimaced. "It's after nine. Maybe we should call it a night."

She nodded and slipped the envelope back in the drawer. "You're right. It is getting late, and I've taken up enough of your time."

"I don't mind," Dwaine was quick to say. "This whole missing doll thing has piqued my interest. I'm in it till the end."

"If there is an end." Sheila scooted her chair away from the desk and stood. "Since you have no record of the doll ever being here, and we don't know for sure if Grandma even brought it into this shop, I fear my Bye-Lo baby might never be found."

The look of defeat on Sheila's face tore at Dwaine's heartstrings. She'd come all the way from California and used vacation time, and he hated to see her go home empty-handed. He took hold of her hand. "I'm not ready to give up yet. I can check with the other antique shops in town and see if they know anything about the doll."

Her blue eyes brightened, although he noticed a few tears on her lashes. "You'd take that much time away from your

business to look for my doll?"

"Searching for treasures is my job."

"Oh, that's right."

He squeezed her fingers. "Why don't you go back to your grandmother's and get a good night's sleep? In the morning, you can come back here and we'll search some more."

She drew in a deep breath. "I'd like that, but I'm not staying with Grandma. I'm staying at a hotel."

"How come?"

"Her apartment at the retirement center is too small. She only has one bedroom."

"But you have other relatives in town, right?"

She nodded. "Jessica and Aunt Marlene. Jessica's painting her kitchen right now, and I'm allergic to paint. And Aunt Marlene is out of town on a cruise."

"Guess a hotel is the best bet for you, then, huh?"

"Yes, and since I'll only be here a short time and got a good deal on the room, I'm fine with it."

He grinned at her. "Great. I'll look forward to seeing you tomorrow, then, Sheila."

"Yes. Tomorrow."

CHAPTER 4

*S*heila stood at her second-floor hotel window, staring at the parking lot. She'd slept better last night than she thought she would, going to bed with confidence that her doll would be found. Dwaine had assured her he would locate the missing doll, and for some reason, she believed him. The new owner of The Older the Better seemed honest and genuinely interested in helping her.

Sheila crammed her hands into the pockets of her fuzzy pink robe. *Of course, he could just be in it for the money. Dwaine did tell me the Bye-Lo baby is worth several hundred dollars.*

The telephone rang, and she jumped. Who would be calling her at nine o'clock in the morning? She grabbed the receiver on the next ring. "Hello."

"Sheila, honey, it's Grandma."

"Oh, hi."

"I didn't wake you, did I?"

"No, I was up. Sorry I didn't get by your place last night to drop off the house key. I'll come by later today, okay?"

"No hurry, dear. You'll be here a week and might want to visit the old place again."

Sheila's gaze went to the Bible Dwaine had found. She'd set it on the nightstand by her bed. "Grandma, Dwaine found a Bible on top of the piano yesterday. Would you like me to bring that by when I drop off the key?"

"An *old* Bible?"

"Yes, it's black and kind of tattered."

"That belonged to your grandpa. Guess it didn't get packed. Would you like to have it, Sheila?"

"Don't you want to keep it?"

"Since you haven't been able to locate the Bye-Lo doll, I'd like you to have the Bible."

"I'd be honored to have Grandpa's Bible, but I'm still going to keep looking for the doll."

"That's fine, dear. Speaking of the doll. . . What did you and that nice young man find out yesterday?" Grandma asked. "Did you find a receipt?"

Sheila blanched. How did Grandma know she and Dwaine had spent time together searching for anything that might give some clue as to what had happened to her Bye-Lo baby?

"Sheila, are you still there?"

"Yes, I'm here." Sheila licked her lips. "How did you know I was looking for the doll with the owner of The Older the Better?"

"He called me yesterday afternoon. Said the two of you were going through some papers in his shop."

"It must have been while he was in the back room," Sheila said. "I never heard him call you."

Grandma sneezed and coughed a few times, and Sheila felt immediate concern. "Are you okay? You aren't coming down with a cold, I hope."

She could hear Grandma blowing her nose. "I'm fine. Just my allergies acting up. I think I'm allergic to the new carpet in my apartment here."

Sheila's heart twisted. Grandma shouldn't have been forced to leave the home she loved and move to some cold apartment in a retirement center where the carpet made her sneeze.

"Why don't you come back to Fresno with me for a while?" Sheila suggested. "I live all alone in Mom and Dad's big old house, and if you like it there, you can stay permanently."

"Oh no! I could never move from Casper." There was a pause. "It's kind of you to offer though."

Sheila understood why Grandma had declined. Her roots went deep, as she'd been born and raised in Casper, Wyoming. She had married and brought her children up here as well. Besides, Grandma probably wouldn't be able to adjust to the heat in California, especially during the summer months.

"I understand," Sheila said, "but please feel free to come visit anytime you like."

"Yes, I will." Another pause. "Now back to that young man who's helping you look for my old doll. . . ."

"What did Dwaine want when he called you?" Sheila asked.

"Dwaine?"

"The new owner of The Older the Better."

"Oh. I think he did tell me his name, but I must have forgotten it."

Sheila dropped to the bed. So Grandma *was* getting forgetful. Maybe she had taken the doll to some other place. Or maybe Bye-Lo was still in her grandmother's possession.

"How come Dwaine phoned you?" Sheila asked again.

Grandma cleared her throat. "He said you and he were going to eat supper together."

"He called to tell you that?"

"Where did you go, dear?"

"To Casper's Café. It's near his shop."

"How nice. I was hoping you would get out and have a little fun while you're here."

Sheila stifled a yawn. "Grandma, I didn't come back to Casper to have fun. I came to choose something from your attic, remember?"

"Yes, of course, but you're twenty-six years old and don't even have a serious boyfriend." Grandma clucked her tongue. "Why, when I was your age, I was already married and had three children."

"Grandma, I'm fine. I enjoy being single." *Liar. I almost married Kevin and was looking forward to raising a family someday.*

Sheila gripped the phone cord in her right hand. "I don't want to spend the rest of my life alone, but the Lord hasn't brought the right man into my life." *And maybe He never will.*

"You might be too fussy," Grandma said. "Did you ever think about that?"

Sheila swallowed hard. Maybe she was. She'd had many dates over the years, but except for Kevin, she'd had no serious relationships.

She shook her head, trying to clear away the troubling thoughts. "Grandma, why did Dwaine really phone? I'm sure it wasn't to inform you that he and I planned to grab a bite of dinner at Casper's Café."

"Supper, dear. We call it supper around here."

Sheila blew out her breath. "Supper then."

"Let's see. . . I believe he called to ask me some questions about the doll."

Sheila's hopes soared. "Did you remember something that might be helpful?" She didn't recall Dwaine saying anything about his call to Grandma. Surely if he'd discovered some helpful information, he would have told her.

Grandma released a sigh. "I'm afraid not, but he did say he was looking for a receipt."

Sheila jumped off the bed and strode back to the window as an idea popped into her head. "What about your copy of the receipt, Grandma? Didn't Bill Summers give you one when you took the doll in?"

"Hmm. . ." Sheila could almost see her grandmother's expression—dark eyebrows drawn together, forehead wrinkled under her gray bangs, and pink lips pursed in contemplation.

"I suppose I did get a receipt," Grandma admitted, "but I have no idea where I put it. With the mess of moving and all,

it could be almost anywhere."

"I see." Sheila couldn't hide her disappointment.

"I've got a suggestion."

"What's that, Grandma?"

"Why don't you go over to The Older the Better again today? You're good at organizing and might be able to help find it."

"I doubt that." Sheila had already spent several hours in Dwaine's shop. The place was a disaster, with nothing organized or filed in the way she would have done had she been running the place.

"Besides," Grandma added, "it will give you a chance to get to know Dwaine better. He's single, you know. Told me so on the phone yesterday."

Sheila's gaze went to the ceiling. Grandma was such a romantic. She remembered how her grandmother used to talk about fixing candlelight dinners for her and Grandpa. Grandma delighted in telling her granddaughters how she believed love and romance were what kept a marriage alive. "That and having the good Lord in the center of your lives," she had said more than once.

Sheila reflected on a special day when Grandma had taken her, Kimber, Lauren, and Jessica shopping. The girls had just been starting into their teen years, and Grandma had bought them each a bottle of perfume, some nail polish, and a tube of lipstick. Then she'd told them how important it was to always look their best in public.

"You never know when you might meet Mr. Right,"

Grandma had said with a wink. As they drove home that day, Grandma had sung "Some Enchanted Evening."

"Sheila, are you still there?"

Grandma's question drove Sheila's musings to the back of her mind. "Yes, and I will go back to the antique shop today," she replied. "But please don't get any ideas about Dwaine Woods becoming my knight in shining armor."

"Of course not, dear. I'll let you make that decision."

Dwaine whistled as he polished a brass vase that had been brought in last week. It was an heirloom and would sell for a tidy sum if he could find the right buyer. He hoped it would be soon, because business had been slow the last few weeks, and he needed to make enough money to pay the bills that were due.

If I could find that Bye-Lo doll for Sheila, I might have the money I need.

A verse—1 Timothy 6:10—popped into Dwaine's head. *"For the love of money is a root of all kinds of evil."*

"I don't really love money, Lord. I just need enough to pay the bills."

Then *"My God will meet all your needs according to the riches of his glory in Christ Jesus,"* from Philippians 4:19, came to mind.

Dwaine placed the vase on a shelf by the front door. He'd done the best he could with it and knew it would sell in God's time. And if he found Sheila's doll, it would be because he was

trying to help, not trying to make a profit at her expense.

An image of the dark-haired beauty flashed into his head. Sheila fascinated him, and if she lived in Casper, he would probably make a move toward a relationship with her.

But she lives in California, he reminded himself. *She'll be leaving soon, so I shouldn't allow myself to get emotionally involved with a woman I may never see again.*

The silver bell above the front entrance jingled as the door swung open. Sheila stepped into the store, looking even more beautiful than she had the day before.

Dwaine's palms grew sweaty, and he swallowed hard. So much for his resolve.

"Hi, Sheila. It's good to see you again."

CHAPTER 5

Sheila halted when she stepped through the door. Dwaine stood beside a shelf a few feet away, holding a piece of cloth and looking at her in a most peculiar way.

"Good morning," she said, trying to ignore his piercing gaze. *Is my lipstick smudged? Could I have something caught between my teeth?*

"You look well rested." He smiled, and she felt herself begin to relax.

"The bed wasn't as comfortable as my own, but at least I slept."

"That's usually the way it is. Hotel beds never measure up to one's own mattress."

Dwaine's dark eyes held her captive, and Sheila had to look away.

"Have you had breakfast yet?" he asked. "I've got some cinnamon rolls and coffee in the back room."

"Thanks, but the hotel served a continental breakfast." She took a step forward. "I dropped by to see if you've had any luck locating the Bye-Lo doll or at least a receipt."

"Sorry, but I haven't had time to look this morning." He nodded toward a brass vase on the shelf. "I started my day by getting out some items I acquired a few weeks ago."

Sheila struggled to keep her disappointment from showing. "I suppose I could go visit Grandma or my cousin Jessica, then check back with you later on." She turned toward the door, but Dwaine touched her shoulder.

"Why don't you stick around awhile? I'll give you more boxes to go through, and while you're doing that, I can finish up with what I'm doing here."

She turned around. "You wouldn't mind me snooping through your things?"

Dwaine leaned his head back and released a chuckle that vibrated against the knotty pine walls.

"What's so funny?"

"When you said 'snooping through my things,' I had this vision of you dressed as Sherlock Holmes, scrutinizing every nook and cranny while looking for clues that might incriminate me."

Sheila snickered. "Right. That's me—Miss Private Eye of the West."

"I know we covered quite an area yesterday," Dwaine said, "but there are a lot of boxes in the back room, not to mention two old steamer trunks. If you'd like to start there, I'll keep working in this room, trying to set out a few more things to sell."

"Sounds like a plan." Sheila shrugged out of her jacket and hung it on the coat tree near the front door.

Dwaine nodded toward the back room. "Don't forget about the coffee and cinnamon rolls, in case you change your mind and decide you're hungry."

"Thanks." Sheila headed to the other room as the bell rang, indicating a customer had come in. She glanced over her shoulder and saw an elderly man holding a cardboard box in his hands.

"Here, let me help you with that." Dwaine took the box from the gray-haired man who'd entered his shop and placed it on the counter.

The man's bushy gray eyebrows drew together. "My wife died six months ago, and I've been going through her things." His blue eyes watered, and he sniffed as though trying to hold back tears.

"I'm sorry about your wife, Mr.—"

"Edwards. Sam Edwards." He thrust out his wrinkled hand, and Dwaine reached across the counter to shake it.

"My wife had a thing for old dolls," Sam went on to say. "I have no use for them, and I could use some extra money. If you think they're worth anything and want to buy 'em, that is."

Dwaine rummaged through the box, noting there were

three dolls with composition heads and bodies, two wooden-ball-jointed bodies with bisque heads, and an old rubber doll that looked like it was ready for burial. He was sure there was some value in the old dolls—all except the one made of rubber. He could probably make a nice profit if he had the dolls fixed, then sold them at the next doll show held in the area. Still, the dolls might be heirlooms, and he would hate to sell anything that should remain in someone's family.

"Don't you have children or grandchildren who might want your wife's dolls?" Dwaine asked.

Sam shook his head. "Wilma and I never had any kids, and none of my nieces seemed interested when I asked them."

"How much are you needing for the dolls?" Dwaine asked, knowing there would be some cost for the repairs, and he might not get his money back if he paid too much for them.

"A hundred dollars would be fine—if you think that's not too high."

Dwaine shook his head. "Actually, I was thinking maybe two hundred."

Sam's eyebrows lifted. "You mean it?"

"Two hundred sounds fair to me."

"All right then."

Dwaine paid the man, escorted him to the front door, and went back to inspect the dolls now in his possession.

"How's it going?" Sheila asked as she entered the room an hour later. "Are you getting lots done?"

He shrugged. "Not really. A man brought in this box of dolls that belonged to his late wife. I've been trying to decide how much each is worth, which ones will need fixing before I can resell them, and which ones to pitch."

"You wouldn't throw out an old doll!" Sheila looked at him as though he'd pronounced a death sentence on someone.

She hurried over to the counter before Dwaine had a chance to respond. "May I see them?" she asked.

He stepped aside. "Be my guest."

Sheila picked up the rubber doll first. It had seen better days, although she thought there might be some hope for it. The head was hard plastic and marred with dirt, but it wasn't broken. The rubber body was cracked in several places, and a couple of fingers and toes were missing. Sheila didn't know much about doll repairs, but it was obvious the rubber body could not be repaired.

"The ball-jointed dolls need restringing, and all the composition ones could use a new paint job," Dwaine said. "I don't see any hope for the rubber one though."

"But the head's in good shape. Couldn't a new body be made to replace the rotting rubber?" Sheila loved dolls and hated the thought of this one ending up in the garbage.

"Replace it with another rubber body, you mean?"

She shook her head. "I was thinking maybe a cloth one. Even if you could find another rubber body, it would probably be in the same shape as this one."

"My sister lives in Seattle, and there's a doll hospital there. I could take these when I visit Eileen next month for Easter."

Dwaine smiled. "Our family always gets together at Easter time to celebrate Christ's resurrection and share a meal together."

Sheila thought about all the Easter dinners she and her family had spent at Grandma and Grandpa Dunmore's over the years. She missed those times, and now that Mom and Dad were on the mission field, unless she went to San Diego to be with her brother, she'd be spending Easter alone.

Dwaine closed the lid on the cardboard box. "I'll worry about these later. Right now, let's see if we can locate your Bye-Lo baby. Unless you've already found something in the back room, that is."

She released a sigh. "Afraid not. I did manage to tidy up the place a bit though."

"You organized?"

Was he irritated with her, or just surprised?

"A little. I took a marking pen and wrote a list of the contents on each box. Then I placed the boxes along one wall, in alphabetical order. I also went through the old trunks, but there was nothing in those except some ancient-looking clothes, which I hung on hangers I found in one of the boxes." She took a quick breath. "I hung the clothes on the wall pegs, and that might help take some of the wrinkles out."

Dwaine released a low whistle. "You've been one busy lady!"

She wondered if he was pleased with her organizational skills or perturbed with her meddling. "I hope you don't mind."

He shook his head. "What's to mind? Your offer to snoop has helped get me more structured. At least in the back room."

He nodded toward the front of his shop. "This part still needs a lot of help."

"I'd be glad to come by anytime during my stay in Casper and help you clean and organize."

Dwaine tipped his head to one side. "You're too good to be true, Sheila Nickels."

"I just like to organize."

"I'm glad someone does." He made a sweeping gesture with his hand. "As you can probably tell, neatness isn't my specialty. Guess I'm more comfortable in chaos."

She shrugged but made no comment.

"I think I'll check one more spot for a receipt," Dwaine said. "Then I say we take a break for some lunch."

Sheila had to admit she was kind of hungry. "That sounds fine."

Dwaine marched across the room, pulled open the bottom drawer of a metal filing cabinet, and rummaged through its contents.

Sheila stood to one side, watching the proceedings and itching to start organizing the files alphabetically.

"Bingo!" Dwaine held up a receipt and smiled. "This has got to be it, Sheila."

She studied the piece of paper and read the scrawled words out loud. "Bye-Lo doll, in good condition: Sold to Weber's Antiques, 10 South Union Avenue, Casper, Wyoming." Sheila frowned. "There's no date, so we don't know when Bill Summers sold Grandma's doll."

Dwaine scratched the side of his head. "How about we

take a ride over to Weber's? It's on the other side of town, and there's a good hamburger place nearby."

"Why not just phone them?"

He shook his head. "It'll be better if we go in person. That way, if Tom Weber doesn't still have the doll, you can show him the picture you have, and he'll know if that's the same doll we're looking for."

Sheila blew out an exasperated breath. "Of course it's the same doll." She pointed to the receipt in his hands. "It says right here that it's a Bye-Lo."

He nodded. "True, but it might not be the same one your grandmother sold to Bill Summers."

She shrugged. "Okay, let's go find out."

CHAPTER 6

Sheila leaned her elbows on the table and scowled at the menu in front of her. They'd paid a visit to Weber's Antique Shop but had come up empty-handed. After looking at the receipt Dwaine showed him and checking his own records, Tom Weber had informed them he'd received a Bye-Lo doll several months ago but had sold it to a doll collector in town. He'd been kind enough to give them the woman's address, and Dwaine had eagerly agreed to drive over to Mrs. Davis's place to see if she had the doll. After going there, Dwaine had suggested they stop for a bite to eat.

"I can see by the scowl on your face that you're fretting about the doll and the fact we still haven't found it."

Dwaine's statement jolted Sheila out of her contemplations. "I was just thinking we're no further ahead than

when we first started."

He shook his head. "I don't see it that way. We found a receipt for a Bye-Lo doll, discovered it had been sold to Weber's Antiques, who in turn sold it to Mrs. Davis, who said she'd originally planned to make new clothes for it and then sell it at the next doll show she went to."

"Then she ended up giving it to her niece for her birthday, but the girl's in school right now so we can't even check on that lead." Sheila pursed her lips as she thought about how much Grandma's doll meant to her. However, she wasn't sure she could take the doll away from a child, even though she would be offering payment.

Dwaine reached for his glass of iced tea. "Let's eat lunch and get to know each other better; then we'll drive over to Amy Davis's house at three thirty, which is when her aunt said she should be home from school."

"I suppose we could do that, but it's only one now. What do we do between the time we finish eating and three thirty?"

"How about we return to my shop, where I can wait for potential customers and you can do more organizing?" He wiggled his eyebrows. "My place is such a mess, and you've done a great job so far in helping get things straightened out."

She smiled in spite of her disappointment over not yet finding Grandma's doll. She had made Dwaine's antique shop look better, and if given the chance, she probably could put the whole place in order.

Dwaine whistled as he washed the front window of his store.

It was more enjoyable to clean and organize when he had help. Sheila was at the back of the store, putting some old books in order according to the authors' last names. Dwaine thought it was kind of silly, since this wasn't the public library, but if it made her happy, he was okay with the idea. Besides, it allowed him more time to be with her. He didn't think it was merely Sheila's dark, curly hair and luminous blue eyes that had sparked his interest either. His attraction to Sheila went much deeper than her physical beauty. She was a Christian, which was the most important thing. Dwaine knew dating a nonbeliever was not in God's plan.

When he heard Sheila singing "Jesus Loves Me," Dwaine smiled and hummed along. When the song ended, he shook his head. *She and I are complete opposites. She likes to organize; I'm a slob. She says "dinner"; I say "supper." She's from sunny California; I'm from windy Wyoming. Still, during the time we've spent together, she has made me feel so complete.*

The grandfather clock struck three, and Dwaine set his roll of paper towels and bottle of cleaner aside. "I think we should head over to Amy Davis's place," he called to Sheila. "She should be home from school by the time we get there."

Sheila strolled across the room. "Are you sure you have time for this, Dwaine? If you keep closing your shop, you might lose all your customers."

He shook his head. "Nah, I'll leave a note saying what time I plan to return, and they'll come back if they were here for anything important."

She eyed him curiously. "Don't you worry about money?"

He shrugged. "It does help pay the bills, but I've come to realize money can't be my primary concern."

"Why are you in business for yourself then?"

"I like what I do." He smiled. "And if I can make a fairly decent living, that's all that matters."

"But you won't even do that if you keep closing your shop."

"Not to worry, Sheila. I'm enjoying the time spent with you."

She blushed. "At first I thought you were only helping me so you could make some money, but since the doll's not in your shop, if we do find her, there's really nothing in it for you."

He grabbed his jacket off the coat tree. "What can I say? I'm just a nice guy trying to help a damsel in distress."

Sheila climbed the steep steps leading to the home of Amy Davis. It was a grand old place and reminded her of Grandma's house. A small balcony protruded from the second floor, and Sheila couldn't help wondering if that might be Amy's room. *Any girl would love to have a balcony off her bedroom. I know I would.*

When Sheila heard a *thunk*, she glanced over her shoulder. To her shock, she discovered Dwaine lying on the bottom step, holding his leg. Her heart lurched, and she rushed to his side. "What happened?"

He groaned. "I was so intent on looking at Mrs. Davis's historical-looking house that I wasn't watching where I was going and missed a step. Fell flat, and I think I sprained my ankle."

Sheila felt immediate concern when she looked at his ankle, already starting to swell. "If you hadn't been traipsing all over town trying to help me find my grandmother's doll, this never would have happened. What if it's broken? What if you can't work because of the fall?"

Dwaine smiled, even though he was obviously in pain. "I'm sure it's not broken, and it's definitely not your fault." He winced as he tried to stand.

"Here, let me help you." Sheila offered her arm, and Dwaine locked his elbow around hers. "I'd better drive you to the hospital so you can have that ankle x-rayed."

He shook his head. "Not yet."

"What do you mean, not yet? In case it is broken, you need immediate care."

"Just help me to the car. I'll wait there while you speak to Amy Davis."

"Are you kidding me? I can't leave you alone while I go running off to see about a doll that might never be mine."

He hopped on one foot and opened the car door on the passenger's side. "We're here, it's three thirty, and you need to know once and for all if your grandmother's doll is still around."

"But Amy might not want to part with it, and I can't fault her for that."

Dwaine slid into the seat and grimaced. "Ouch."

"Are you sure you're going to be okay?"

"I'll be fine. Now please go knock on the door and find out if the doll's here or not."

Sheila looked up at the stately home, then back at Dwaine again, and sighed. "I'll only be a few minutes, and as soon as I'm done, we're going to the hospital."

He saluted her. "Whatever you say, ma'am."

Sheila closed the car door and made her way up the long flight of stairs. *I'm surprised it wasn't me who fell. I was studying this grand home, too, and it could have been my ankle that was injured instead of Dwaine's.*

A few seconds later, she stood on the front porch and rang the doorbell. While she waited, she glanced down at her rental car. At least Dwaine hadn't wasted his gasoline on this trip.

Finally, the door opened and a middle-aged woman with light brown hair greeted her with a smile. "May I help you?"

"I'm looking for Amy Davis."

"I don't believe I've met you before. Do you know my daughter?"

Sheila extended her hand. "I'm Sheila Nickels, and I'm in Casper visiting my grandmother who lives at Mountain Springs Retirement Center."

The woman shook Sheila's hand, but her wrinkled forehead revealed obvious confusion. "I'm not sure what that has to do with Amy."

Sheila quickly explained about her visit to Grandma's attic, the missing Bye-Lo doll, and how she and Dwaine had gotten Amy's name and address.

"Let me get this straight," Mrs. Davis said. "You believe the doll Amy's aunt gave her might actually be your grandmother's doll?"

"Yes, I think it's quite possible."

Mrs. Davis opened the door wider. "Please, come in."

Sheila took one last look at the car. She could see Dwaine leaning against the headrest, and a wave of guilt washed over her. She should be driving him to the hospital now, not taking time to see about a doll. *But I'm here,* she reminded herself, *and Dwaine insisted he was okay, so I may as well see what I can find out.*

"Have a seat in the living room and I'll get my daughter." Mrs. Davis ascended the stairs just off the hallway, while Sheila meandered into the other room and positioned herself on the couch. It was near the front window, so she could keep an eye on Dwaine. *I hope his leg's not broken, and I pray he isn't in much pain.* Sheila hated to admit it, but the carefree antique dealer was working his way into her heart, even though she'd only met him yesterday. It wasn't like her to have strong feelings for someone she barely knew. She, who had kept her heart well guarded since her broken engagement to Kevin.

Sheila heard the floor creak, and she snapped her attention away from the window, turning toward the noise. A teenaged girl with hazel-colored eyes and long blond hair gazed at her with a curious expression. "I'm Amy Davis. My mother said you wanted to speak to me and that you were interested in the doll my aunt gave me for my birthday."

Sheila nodded. "Yes, that's right."

"I hope you're not planning to take the Bye-Lo away, because I collect dolls, and she's special to me."

"I—I just want to see her. I need to know if she's the same

150

doll my grandma used to have in her attic." Sheila didn't have the heart to tell Amy that if it was Grandma's doll, she planned to offer payment to get it back.

"Hang on a minute." Amy whirled around and hurried out of the room. A short time later she was back, holding a small cardboard box in her hands. She set it on the coffee table in front of the couch and opened the lid. Carefully, almost reverently, she lifted the doll and cradled it in her arms as though it were a real baby.

Sheila's heart hammered. It sure looked like Grandma's doll. It was the same size and had the exact shade of brown painted on its pink porcelain head, and the doll's hands were made of celluloid. "May I have a closer look?"

With a reluctant expression, Amy handed Sheila the doll. "Be careful with her. She's breakable."

"Yes, I know." Sheila placed the Bye-Lo baby in her lap and lifted her white nightgown.

"What are you doing?" Amy's eyes were huge, and she looked horror-struck.

"I want to see if there's any writing on her tummy."

Amy dropped to the couch beside Sheila. "Why would there be writing? I never wrote anything on the doll."

"If this is my grandmother's, then my name should be on the stomach. I wrote it there when I was a little girl, hoping someday the doll would be mine." Sheila pulled the small flannel diaper aside, but there was no writing. Part of her felt a sense of relief. At least she wouldn't be faced with having to ask Amy to give up a doll she obviously cared about. Another part of her was sad. Since this wasn't Grandma's doll, then where was she?

Sheila smoothed the clothes back into place and handed the Bye-Lo to Amy. "It's not my grandmother's doll, and I apologize for having troubled you."

Amy's mother stepped into the room just then. "It was no bother." She walked Sheila to the door. "I hope you find your grandmother's doll. I suspect it meant a lot to you."

Sheila could only nod in reply, for she was afraid if she spoke she might break down in tears. It was clear she wasn't going to locate the missing doll, and now she had to take Dwaine to the hospital to have his ankle checked out. All she'd accomplished today was getting Dwaine hurt and making herself feel more depressed. *Maybe I never should have come back to Casper. Maybe I'm not supposed to have that doll.*

CHAPTER 7

For the next week, Sheila divided her time between Mountain Springs Retirement Center, to see Grandma, and The Older the Better Antique Shop, to help Dwaine. After his ankle had been x-rayed, the doctor determined that it wasn't broken but he'd sprained it badly. Dwaine would be hobbling around on crutches for a couple of weeks, which would make it difficult to wait on customers, much less stock shelves, clean, or organize things in his shop. Since Sheila felt responsible for the accident, she'd called her boss and asked if she could take her last two weeks of vacation now. Dr. Taylor agreed, saying the woman he'd hired in Sheila's absence was available to help awhile longer and telling Sheila to enjoy the rest of her time off. Since Sheila couldn't afford another week or two at a hotel, after speaking with Grandma, she decided to stay in her grandmother's old house until she felt ready to leave Casper. There was still enough furniture for her to get by, and since the power was on, she figured she could manage okay.

"This is so much fun," she muttered under her breath as she dumped another load of trash into the wastebasket near Dwaine's desk. Every day this week when she'd been helping Dwaine, Sheila had continued to search for Grandma's doll or a receipt. No amount of cleaning or organizing revealed any evidence that the doll had ever been in Dwaine's store. Dwaine had phoned all the other antique shops in town, but no one had any record of her grandmother's doll. Sheila felt sure it was hopeless.

"I'd like to meet your grandmother in person and ask a few more questions about the doll," Dwaine said as he hobbled up to Sheila on his crutches.

"That's a great idea. Grandma's been wanting to meet you, and I happen to know she baked a batch of peanut butter cookies yesterday afternoon."

He wiggled his eyebrows. "One of my all-time favorites."

Sheila smiled at Dwaine's enthusiasm. He reminded her of a little boy. During the past week, she'd gotten to know him better. His lackadaisical attitude and disorganization bothered her some, but he had a certain charm that captivated her. Not only was Dwaine good looking, but he seemed so kind and compassionate. Several times she'd seen him deal with customers, and always he'd been polite and fair in his business dealings. Even though Sheila knew little about antiques, she could tell by the customers' reactions how pleased they were

with the prices he quoted.

"So when do we leave?"

Dwaine's question halted Sheila's musings, and she gazed up at him. "Oh, you mean go to Grandma's place?"

He nodded and grinned at her. "That's where the peanut butter cookies are, right?"

"Yes. I just didn't realize you wanted to go there this minute."

"Business has been slow this morning, so there's no time like the present."

Sheila was tempted to say something about Dwaine's overly casual manner, but she decided it was none of her business how he handled things at his shop.

He made his way across the room and reached for his jacket. In the process, the coat tree nearly fell over, and Sheila was afraid Dwaine might lose his balance, too. With one hand she grabbed the wobbly object; with the other she took hold of Dwaine's arm. "Better let me help you with your jacket."

As soon as they had their coats on, she opened the front door, stepped outside, and headed for her rental.

"I've always wondered how it would feel to have a chauffeur," Dwaine said in a teasing voice. "Since I sprained my ankle, it's been kind of nice having you drive me around."

Dwaine had never been to Mountain Springs Retirement Center, but when they pulled into the parking lot, he was impressed with the facilities. The grounds were well cared for and included numerous picnic tables, wooden benches, bird feeders, and a couple of birdbaths.

When they entered the building, he noticed the foyer was decorated with several green plants, and a huge fish tank was built into one wall.

Sheila led the way, walking slowly down a long corridor and up the elevator to the third floor. Soon they were standing in front of a door with Lydia Dunmore's name engraved on a plaque.

A few minutes after Sheila knocked, the door opened. A slightly plump elderly woman with her hair styled in a short bob greeted them with a smile. Her blue eyes sparkled, the same way Sheila's did, and she held out her arms. "Sheila, what a nice surprise!"

Sheila giggled and embraced the woman. "Grandma, you know I've dropped by here nearly every day since I came back to Casper. I don't see how my being here now can be such a surprise."

"Of course not, dear, but this is the first time you've shown up with a man at your side." She glanced over at Dwaine and smiled. "And such a nice-looking one, too."

Dwaine's ears burned from her scrutiny, and he noticed Sheila's face had turned crimson as well.

"Grandma, this is Dwaine Woods, the new owner of The Older the Better Antique Shop."

"It's nice to meet you in person. I'm Lydia Dunmore." She held out her hand.

Dwaine was surprised at the strength of Lydia's handshake.

"It's good to meet you, Mrs. Dunmore."

"Lydia. Please call me Lydia."

He nodded in reply.

"Sheila told me about your ankle. How are you doing?"

"Getting along quite well, thanks to your granddaughter helping out at my shop."

"Glad to hear that. So now, to what do I owe the privilege of this visit?" she asked, motioning them inside her apartment.

"I heard you made some cookies," Dwaine blurted.

Sheila nudged him gently in the ribs. "I can't believe you said that."

"Me neither." Dwaine shook his head. "The words slipped out before I had time to think. Sorry about that, Mrs.—I mean, Lydia."

She chuckled and headed for the small kitchen area. "You remind me of my late husband. He always said exactly what was on his mind."

Sheila pulled out a wooden stool at the snack bar for Dwaine and took his crutches, placing them nearby. "Have a seat. Grandma loves to entertain, so I'm sure she can't wait to serve us."

Sheila studied Dwaine's profile as he leaned his elbows on the counter and made easy conversation with Grandma.

"Yes, ma'am," he said in answer to Grandma's most recent question. "I've gone to church ever since I was a boy. Accepted the Lord as my Savior when I was a teenager, and now I teach a teen Sunday school class."

Grandma piled a plate high with peanut butter cookies and placed it in front of Dwaine. Then she poured a tall glass of milk and handed it to him.

"Hey, don't I get any?" Sheila stuck out her lower lip in an exasperated pout.

"Don't worry your pretty little head." Grandma put half as many cookies on another plate, poured a second glass of milk, and handed them to Sheila.

Before Sheila could voice the question, Grandma said, "What can I say? He's a growing boy with a sprained ankle and needs more cookies than you do."

Dwaine patted his stomach. "If I'm not careful, I'll be growing fat."

"You could use a little more meat on your bones." Grandma glanced at Sheila. "Don't you think so, dear?"

Sheila's face flamed. She thought Dwaine looked fine the way he was. A bit too fine, maybe. She sure wasn't going to admit that to her grandmother though.

Searching for a change of subject, Sheila said, "Dwaine and I have looked high and low for anything that would show you took the Bye-Lo doll to his shop, but we haven't found a thing."

Grandma tipped her head to one side. "Guess you'd better make another trip to my attic."

"I appreciate the offer, but as I told you before, there's nothing else I want." Sheila took a bite of her cookie. "Mmm. . .this is good."

"Thanks." Grandma grinned and snatched a cookie from Sheila's plate. "I'm glad you two stopped by so I didn't have to eat them all myself."

"I was wondering if you've had the chance to look at my appraisal of your piano," Dwaine said.

Grandma's forehead wrinkled. "Your offer sounds fair, Dwaine, but to tell you the truth, I'm having a hard time parting with that old relic. I've had it since I was a girl."

Dwaine swallowed the last of his milk. "Too bad there isn't room for it here."

Tears welled up in Grandma's eyes. "Even if I could have had it moved to this apartment, I don't think the others who live here would appreciate my playing it. These walls aren't soundproof, you know."

"There's a piano downstairs in the game room," Sheila said. "Grandma can play that whenever she wants."

"Maybe someone in your family would like to buy the piano," Dwaine said.

Grandma smiled. "I'll have to ask around."

Dwaine looked at Sheila. "One good thing has come from hunting for the missing doll."

"Oh, what's that?"

"I've gotten to know you."

"The man has a point," Grandma put in. "I can tell by the way you two look at each other that you're a match made in heaven."

"Grandma, please!" Sheila knew her face must be bright red, because she felt heat travel up the back of her neck and cascade onto her cheeks.

"You look a little flushed, dear. I hope you're not coming down with something."

"I think Sheila's embarrassed by your last statement," Dwaine said, coming to Sheila's rescue.

Grandma looked sheepish. "Sorry about that."

"Dwaine and I barely know each other," Sheila said. "I think you're a romantic at heart, Grandma."

Grandma grinned. "Your grandpa and I got married after knowing each other only one month, and we had a wonderful marriage. It's always been my desire that each of my children and grandchildren find a suitable mate and know the kind of happiness Grandpa and I had." She winked at Dwaine. "Sheila's more priceless than any of my attic treasures, so don't let her get away."

CHAPTER 3

*S*heila and Dwaine drove back to his shop in silence. He was busy writing something in a notebook he'd taken from his jacket pocket, and she needed time to think. Was Grandma right about her and Dwaine? Were they a match made in heaven? Could it be that God had brought Sheila back to Casper to begin a relationship with Dwaine, not for the Bye-Lo baby?

Sheila gripped the steering wheel as a ball of anxiety rolled in the pit of her stomach. *No, it couldn't be. If I allow myself to fall for this man, one of us would have to move. A long-distance relationship won't work. Kevin proved that when he moved to Oregon and sent me a letter saying he'd met someone else.*

As though he sensed she was thinking about him, Dwaine looked over at her and smiled. "It's almost noon, and I'm getting kind of hungry. Should we stop for lunch somewhere?"

Sheila focused on the road ahead. "After all those cookies you ate at Grandma's, I wouldn't think you'd have any room for lunch."

"Aw, those only whetted my appetite."

She snickered. "Yeah, I could tell."

"Seriously, I would like to take you to lunch."

"How about I pay for the meal today? You bought me dinner—I mean, supper—a couple times last week and only let me leave the tip." She clucked her tongue. "And that was just because I threatened to make a scene if you didn't."

Dwaine tapped the notebook against his knee. "You really don't have to even things out. I enjoy your company, and while our meals aren't exactly dates, I find myself wishing they were."

Sheila's heart pounded, and her hands became sweaty. "You do?"

"Yep. In fact, I've been working up the nerve to ask if you'd go out with me."

"You mean something more than supper?"

"Right. A real date, where I come to your grandma's old place and pick you up."

"Where would we go?" Sheila hadn't meant to enjoy his company so much. She'd be leaving Casper soon, and then what?

"I thought maybe we could take in a show. A couple of good movies are playing right now, and tonight there shouldn't be a lot of people."

"But this is Monday—a weeknight," she reminded.

"And?"

"You'll need to get up early tomorrow for work." Sheila was an early to bed, early to rise kind of person, and it was a good thing. Dr. Taylor opened his chiropractic clinic at eight o'clock, five mornings a week, and Sheila had never been late to work.

"I own my own business, which means I can set my own hours," Dwaine replied.

"Still, maybe we should wait until Friday to go out."

"I don't want to wait that long. You'll be leaving for California soon, and we shouldn't waste the time you have left."

Sheila's heart skipped a beat. "You've seen me nearly every day for the last two weeks."

"Those weren't dates. That was business." He touched her arm, and even through her jacket she felt warm tingles.

Sheila stared at the road ahead. She had to keep her focus on driving, not Dwaine. The truth was, except for his disorganization, he had all the attributes she was looking for in a man. Dwaine appeared to be kind, gentle, caring, humorous—and as a bonus, he was good-looking—but most important, he was a Christian.

"You haven't said if you'll go out with me tonight or not," he prompted.

Sheila took a deep breath and threw caution to the wind. "Sure, why not? Since we can't seem to find Grandma's doll, I may as well make good use of my time spent here."

A knock at the door let Sheila know her date had arrived. She took one last look in the hall mirror and hurried to answer it, hoping she looked okay. She'd decided to wear a long black skirt and a pale blue blouse, which she knew brought out the color of her eyes.

When she opened the door, Sheila's breath caught in her throat. Dwaine was dressed in a pair of beige slacks and a black leather jacket, and a bouquet of pink and white carnations was tucked under one arm. "The flowers are for you, pretty lady."

Since Dwaine's hands gripped his crutches, Sheila reached for the bouquet. "Thanks. They're beautiful." She scanned the room, looking for something to put the flowers in. "I'd better get a glass of water from the kitchen. I'm pretty sure Grandma's vases have all been packed away, because I haven't seen any in the kitchen cupboards."

When Sheila returned a few seconds later, she set the glass of water on the small table in the entryway and placed the flowers inside.

"You look beautiful tonight," Dwaine said, offering her a wide smile.

"You don't look so bad yourself."

"Ready to go?"

She nodded and grabbed her coat from the closet, but before she could put it on, Dwaine set his crutches aside and took it from her. "Here, let me help you with that."

"You're going to fall over if you're not careful."

"Nah. I'm gettin' good at doing things on one foot."

As Sheila slipped her arms inside the sleeves, she shivered. "You cold?"

"No, not really." She buttoned the coat and opened the door. "What time does the show start?"

"Not until seven thirty. I thought we'd start with dinner at a nice restaurant, then follow it with the movies."

Sheila snickered. "You just said 'dinner' instead of 'supper.'"

He winked. "This is a date. Gentlemen take their ladies out to dinner, not supper."

Sheila hated to see her date with Dwaine end. Dinner had been delicious, the show had been great, and she'd enjoyed every minute spent in his company. Now they stood on Grandma's front porch, about to say good night.

"I had a good time tonight. Thanks," Sheila said.

"Yeah, me, too." His voice was husky, and his dark eyes held her captive. "How about a drive to the country tomorrow during our lunch break? I can get chicken to go from Casper's Café."

She licked her lips. "That sounds good. I love fried chicken."

There was an awkward pause; then Dwaine lowered his head and his lips sought hers. The kiss was gentle and soft, lasting only a few seconds, but it took Sheila's breath away. Things were happening too fast, and her world was tilting precariously.

"Good night. See you tomorrow," Dwaine murmured before she had a chance to say anything. He hobbled down the steps, leaving Sheila with a racing heart and a head full of tangled emotions as she shut the door.

She'd been caught up in the enjoyment of the evening and had let him kiss her. "I've got to call a halt to this before one of us gets hurt," she mumbled at her reflection in the mirror. "Even though I enjoy Dwaine's company and believe he's a true Christian, a long-distance relationship will never work. I'll tell him in the morning that I'd rather not take a drive to the country."

Somewhere in the distance an annoying bell kept ringing. Pulling herself from the haze of sleep, Sheila slapped her hand on the clock by the antique bed in Grandma's guest room. "It can't be time to get up. It seems like I just went to bed."

The ringing continued, and she finally realized it was the phone and not her alarm. She grabbed for the receiver. "Hello."

"Hi, Sheila, it's Dwaine. When you didn't show up at nine this morning, I started to worry. Are you okay?"

Sheila stifled a yawn and rolled out of bed. "I'm fine." She glanced at the clock and cringed when she realized it was almost ten o'clock. "Sorry, guess I overslept and must have forgotten to set the alarm."

"That's okay, but I've got some news to share when you get here."

"Can't you tell me now? I'm curious." Sheila stretched and reached for her fuzzy pink robe.

"I stayed up last night reading some doll collectors' magazine I recently bought, and I think I may have found your missing doll."

She flopped onto the bed, draping the robe across her legs. "Really? What makes you think it's the one?"

"It fits the description you gave me, and there's some writing on the doll's cloth body. Could be your name, Sheila."

She sucked in her breath. *Maybe the trip to Casper hasn't been a waste of time after all.* Her conscience pricked her. *How could I even think such a thing? Grandma's here, and I've enjoyed spending time with her—Dwaine, too, for that matter.*

"Sheila, are you still there?"

"Yes, yes. You really think you've found my grandma's doll?"

"There's no way to be sure until you take a look at the magazine." There was a brief pause, and Sheila thought she heard the bell above the door of Dwaine's store jingle. "A customer just walked in, so I'd better go," he said. "If you can come over as soon as possible, we'll have time to check out the doll information before we go for our drive."

Sheila clutched the folds in her robe. "About our picnic date—"

"Gotta go. See you soon, Sheila."

There was a click, and the telephone went dead. Sheila blew out her breath and placed the phone back on the table. Even though she was a bit put out with Dwaine for hanging up so abruptly, she felt a sense of elation over the possibility that he might have actually found Grandma's doll.

For the next hour, when Dwaine wasn't waiting on customers, he watched the door, anxious for Sheila to arrive. He was excited to show her the information about the Bye-Lo doll in the magazine he'd found, but more than that, he looked forward to seeing Sheila again. After their date last night, he was convinced he wanted to begin a relationship with her.

Dwaine snapped the cash register drawer shut and shook his head. *This is ridiculous. I can't be falling for someone who lives three states away. Would Sheila be willing to relocate? I don't think I could live in California.*

The bell above the door jingled as one customer left the store and another entered. It was Sheila, wearing a pair of blue jeans with a matching jacket. "Have you got time to show me that doll magazine?" she asked.

"Sure. There's a lull between customers, so come on back." Dwaine motioned for Sheila to follow him over to his desk in one corner of the room. He leaned his crutches against the side of the desk and took a seat. She sat in the straight-backed oak chair nearby.

Dwaine pointed to the magazine. "Here's the Bye-Lo that caught my attention. Don't you think she looks like your grandmother's old doll?"

Sheila jumped out of her chair and leaned over his shoulder. "That does look like her, but I can't be sure. I wish the writing on the doll's stomach was clearer."

Dwaine stared at the picture. "Guess I'd better contact the person who placed this ad and ask what the writing says."

"It might be good to find out how much they're asking for the doll, too." Sheila blew out her breath, and he shivered as it tickled his neck.

168

"I want that doll really bad, but if it's going to cost too much, I may have to pass."

"After all the searching we've done, you can't walk away if this is your grandmother's doll. I'm sure we can work something out."

"I'm serious, Dwaine. Besides paying for the doll, I'll have to cover the cost of your services."

He swiveled his chair, bumping heads with her in the process. "Ouch!"

"I'm so sorry." He wrapped his arms around her, and she fell into his lap.

Sheila let out a gasp, but he covered her mouth with his before she could protest. His lips were soft, warm, and inviting. She responded by threading her fingers through the back of his hair.

Dwaine wished the kiss could have gone on forever, but the spell was broken when another customer entered the store.

Sheila jerked her head back and jumped up. Her face was the shade of a ripe Red Delicious apple.

"I–I'd better get to work. I've got a lot more cleaning to do in the back room." She stumbled away from Dwaine.

"We'll stop work at noon so we can take our drive to the country with a picnic lunch," he called after her.

"I've changed my mind and decided not to go."

The door to the storage room clicked shut before Dwaine could say anything more. He turned to the elderly woman who had entered the shop and forced a smile. "May I help you, ma'am?"

CHAPTER 9

Sheila paced back and forth, from the living room window of Grandma's old house to the couch, still covered by a sheet. She'd left The Older the Better almost two hours ago and hadn't heard a word from Dwaine. He'd said he would call her tonight if he heard from the doll collector.

Of course, she reasoned, *it might take days for him to get a reply about the doll. But I'll be leaving soon, and then what?*

The phone rang in the kitchen, and Sheila rushed out of the room to get it. "Dwaine?" she asked breathlessly into the receiver.

"No, it's Grandma."

"Oh, hi." Sheila stared out the back window into the neighbor's yard. A young couple with a baby was getting into their car. Her heart took a nosedive. Would she ever fall in

love, get married, and have children?

"Sheila, did you hear what I said?"

She jerked her gaze away from the window. "What was that, Grandma?"

"I asked if you would like to have supper at my place tonight with Dwaine."

"Thanks for the invite, but I'm not in the mood to eat with the group at the retirement center."

"I wasn't planning to eat downstairs," Grandma said.

"You weren't?"

"No. I hoped to try out a recipe I found in a magazine, and I wanted to cook it for someone besides myself."

Sheila laughed. "You're needing a guinea pig, huh?"

"Actually, I'd prefer to have two guinea pigs."

Sheila groaned. "Grandma, you're not trying to play matchmaker, are you?"

Grandma cleared her throat and gave a polite little cough. "Of course not, dear. What would give you that idea?"

Sheila thought about telling Grandma how she and Dwaine had made a date for this afternoon and how she'd changed her mind about going. If she invited Dwaine to join her for supper at Grandma's, it would be like sending him mixed signals.

"Sheila, please don't say no. You'll be leaving next week, and I'd like to spend as much time with you as possible before you go." Grandma's tone was kind of pathetic, and Sheila figured she would feel guilty for days if she turned down the invitation.

Sheila shifted the phone from one ear to the other. "Okay, I'll come, but let's make it just the two of us. I'm sure Dwaine is busy."

"No, he's not. I already invited him."

Sheila flopped into the closest chair at the table. "You asked him first?"

There was a pause. "I was afraid you might refuse."

"Dwaine and I aren't right for each other. So you may as well give up your matchmaker plans."

Grandma chuckled. "Who are you trying to convince, sweet girl? Me or yourself?"

"I live in California, and Dwaine lives here in Wyoming. A long-distance relationship would never work."

"One of you could move."

"My job is there, and his is here."

"Have you prayed about this?"

Sheila hated to admit it, but she hadn't. It wasn't like her not to pray about a situation she knew only the Lord could resolve.

Grandma clucked her tongue. "Your silence tells me you probably haven't taken this matter to God. Am I right?"

"Yes, Grandma, you're right."

"I think you're making excuses and should give the situation serious thought, as well as a lot of prayer. Jobs are to be had in every town, you know."

Sheila drew in a deep breath and released it with a moan. "I'll admit, I am attracted to Dwaine, but I don't know why, because we're as different as east is from west."

"How so?"

"For one thing, I'm a neat freak; I'm always organizing."

"I can't argue with that. The last time you dropped by, you organized my kitchen cupboards so well I couldn't find anything for two days."

"According to Dwaine, his shop was a mess when he bought it, but to tell you the truth, I'm not sure he is much better about organization than the previous owner," Sheila said, ignoring her grandmother's teasing comment. "That receipt for your old doll is probably someplace in his shop, and we can't unearth it because of all the clutter."

"I would think with your ability to organize, you'd have found the doll or a receipt if it was still there."

"I've checked everywhere I could think of, and so has Dwaine."

"I'm sorry you came all this way to get one of my attic treasures, and now you'll be going home empty-handed."

"I guess the doll's not really that important, and I do have Grandpa's Bible." As the words slipped off her tongue, Sheila knew she hadn't really meant them. Would she be okay going home without the Bye-Lo baby? Could she return to California and never think of Dwaine Woods again? Would his kisses be locked away in her heart forever?

"Sure wish you'd consider taking something else from the attic," Grandma said. "I could come over to the old house tomorrow and help check things out."

Sheila shook her head, although she didn't know why; Grandma couldn't see the action. "Actually, Dwaine might have another lead on the doll."

"Really? Why didn't you say so before?"

"He found a Bye-Lo baby advertised in a doll collectors' magazine, and it looks like your old doll. There's even some writing on the cloth body, but it could be another false lead."

"Writing? Why would there be writing on the doll?"

Sheila's face heated with embarrassment. She'd been only eight years old when she wrote her name on the doll's stomach, but she'd never told Grandma what she'd done.

"I—uh—am sorry to say that I wrote my name on Bye-Lo's tummy when I was a little girl."

"Whatever for?"

"Because I wanted her to be mine someday, and I hoped maybe. . ." Sheila's voice trailed off.

"Oh, I see."

"It was a stupid, childish thing to do, and I'm sorry, Grandma."

"Apology accepted." Grandma chuckled. "Who knows, your name might be the very thing that helps you know for sure if it's my doll or not."

"That's why I'm hoping the person who placed the ad responds to Dwaine's phone call soon."

"While you're waiting to hear, won't you join me and Dwaine for supper this evening?"

Sheila nearly choked. "He said yes?"

"Sure did. Now how 'bout you, dear? Will you come, too?"

Sheila felt like she was backed into a corner, but she didn't want to disappoint Grandma. "What time should I be there?"

"Six o'clock. Dwaine will pick you up at a quarter to."

"You arranged that as well?" Sheila's voice rose a notch.

"What else are grandmas for?" Grandma giggled like a young girl. "See you tonight, and wear something pretty."

Sheila lifted her gaze toward the ceiling. "Sure, Grandma."

At a quarter to six, Dwaine arrived at Lydia Dunmore's stately old house to pick up Sheila. His ankle felt somewhat better, so he'd left his crutches at home. He lifted his hand to knock on the door, but it swung open before his knuckles connected with the wood.

"I saw you through the peephole," Sheila said before he could voice the question.

"Ah, so you were waiting for me." He chuckled, and she blushed.

"I'll grab my sweater and then we can go." Sheila disappeared into the living room and returned with a fuzzy blue sweater. Instead of blue jeans and a sweatshirt, like she'd had on today, she was dressed in a pale blue dress that touched her ankles.

"I felt bad when you didn't want to drive to the country this afternoon," Dwaine said as they headed down the steps side by side.

She halted when they came to the sidewalk and turned to face him. "I didn't think it was a good idea for us to go on another date."

He opened his mouth to comment, but she cut him off.

"For that matter, I don't think tonight is such a good idea, either, but I'm doing it for Grandma."

A wave of disappointment shot through Dwaine, and he cringed. "Am I that hard to take?"

She shook her head. "Except for our completely opposite ways of doing things, I find you attractive and fun to be with."

"I enjoy your company, too; so what's the problem?"

Sheila held up one finger. "I live in California, and you live here. Not an ideal situation for dating, wouldn't you say?"

He shrugged his shoulders. "I'm sure we can work something out."

She lifted her chin and stared at him. "Are you willing to relocate?"

"I moved from Montana to Wyoming because I like it here. I also like my antique store, and I think in time I'll make a fairly decent living because of it."

"And I have a great job in Fresno," she countered.

Dwaine opened the car door for Sheila, glad he didn't have to share the confines of his compact car with anyone else. He needed this chance to speak with Sheila alone before they headed to her grandmother's retirement center.

When he climbed into the driver's seat and clicked his door shut, Dwaine leaned toward her. "Sheila, I thought we had something going between us, and after that kiss the other night—"

She pulled away. "Can we please change the subject?"

"What do you want to talk about?"

"How about my grandmother's doll? Did you hear from the person who placed the ad in that doll magazine?"

He shook his head. "Nope. They haven't returned my call

or sent any e-mails."

Her eyes clouded with obvious disappointment. "Oh."

Dwaine wanted to pull her into his arms and offer reassurance, but he figured a hug wouldn't be appreciated, and he could tell she didn't want to talk about their relationship. "If I don't hear something by tomorrow, I'll call again," he promised.

"Thanks. I appreciate that."

"This lemon chicken is delicious," Sheila said as she smiled across the table at Grandma.

Dwaine smacked his lips. "I second that, and to prove it, I'll have another piece." He stabbed a chicken leg with his fork and plopped it onto his plate.

"Sheila says you may have found my old doll," Grandma said.

He swallowed the meat he'd put in his mouth before answering. "It's a collector who buys and sells antique dolls."

"I understand there's some writing on the doll's body."

He nodded. "That's how it was stated in the description; only it didn't say what the writing said."

"I can't believe that Sheila doing something as naughty as writing her name on a doll could prove to be helpful years later." Grandma chuckled behind her napkin. "Sheila always was possessive of the doll. I never knew how much until she confessed she'd written her name on its stomach."

Dwaine laughed and shoveled another bite of meat into his mouth.

Sheila gritted her teeth. *The way these two are carrying on, you'd think I wasn't even in the room.*

"Sheila dear, you haven't said more than a few words since we sat down." Grandma wagged her finger.

"I've—uh—been eating."

"She did say she likes your chicken," Dwaine said.

"If you don't mind, I prefer to speak for myself." Sheila's voice sounded harsh, and Grandma and Dwaine looked at her like she'd taken leave of her senses.

"Are you upset about something?" Grandma asked.

Of course Sheila was upset. She'd taken a week's vacation to look for a doll Grandma had apparently sold and no one could find. Then she'd asked her boss for another two weeks so she could continue to search for the doll while helping Dwaine at his shop because he'd sprained his ankle on her account. To make matters worse, every lead they'd had so far had turned up nothing. Unless the magazine ad brought forth helpful information, it was likely Sheila would return to California without her attic treasure. Her final frustration came from falling for a guy who lived hundreds of miles from her.

"Sheila?"

"I'm fine, Grandma. Just tired, I guess."

"I'd like to date your granddaughter," Dwaine blurted, "but she's not interested."

Sheila didn't wait for Grandma's response. She leaped to her feet and raced out of the apartment.

Dwaine limped down the hall after Sheila, his heart pounding and his mind whirling with unanswered questions. She'd acted

strangely all evening, but what had happened to set her off like this?

Dwaine caught up to Sheila as she stepped into the elevator. "Wait!"

The door started to close, but he stuck out his hand and held it open.

"Where do you think you're running off to?" he panted.

Sheila averted her gaze and stared at the floor. "Home. I'm going home."

"But you said you weren't leaving until next week."

She looked up, and her eyelids fluttered. "I'm going back to Grandma's old house, where I won't have to spend the evening being talked *about* rather than *to*."

Dwaine stepped into the elevator and pushed the button so the door would close more quickly. He didn't want to chance her bolting again.

"Ever since we sat down to supper, you and Grandma talked about me like I wasn't even in the room." Sheila's chin quivered. "I'm already upset over not finding the Bye-Lo doll, and I don't like being treated as if I'm a child."

"I'm sorry. I didn't realize that's what I was doing."

Sheila blinked, and a few tears rolled down her cheeks. "That's not all."

"What else is bothering you?"

"I feel like all you care about is going on dates and having fun. Finding my grandmother's doll doesn't seem to be a priority anymore—if it ever was."

He shook his head. "That's not true, Sheila. I told you

179

about the magazine ad, didn't I?"

"Yes, but what have you done to contact the person who placed it?"

"I told you before; I called and left a message on their answering machine." He sighed. "Can't really do much more until I hear back, now, can I?"

She shrugged and hung her head. "I've never run out on Grandma like that before. I don't know what came over me, and I need to go back and apologize."

"I guess it's my fault. I'm the reason you got so upset."

"No, it's my fault. I shouldn't have let myself—"

"I've enjoyed spending time with you these past few weeks, and I hope we can keep in touch after you return home," he interrupted.

The elevator door swished open, and Sheila hurried toward her grandmother's room. Dwaine did his best to keep up, but the pain in his ankle slowed him down.

"I'll give you my e-mail address so you can let me know what you hear on the Bye-Lo baby," she said over her shoulder.

"Right, but I was thinking more along the lines of our keeping in touch so we can build a relationship," he mumbled.

She stopped walking and turned to face him. "Again, I don't see how we can have a relationship when we live in two different states."

He gave her a sheepish grin. "Ah, that. Well, I figure if the Lord brought us together, He will make a way."

CHAPTER 10

_F_heila couldn't believe her vacation was over and she was back in Fresno. Her flight had gone well, and she'd called a cab to drive her home. She should be happy and content, but instead, her heart was filled with a sense of loss that went deeper than just losing a doll. Was it possible she could love Dwaine after knowing him only a few weeks?

The first thing Sheila did when she stepped inside her house was check her e-mail. Sure enough, there was one from Dwaine, entitled "Response from doll collector."

As she read the message, Sheila's heart plummeted. The writing on the doll confirmed that it wasn't Grandma's. As if that wasn't bad enough news, Dwaine didn't even say he would continue to look.

"He did say he misses me," she murmured. "Guess I should

be happy about that."

She glanced around the living room and loneliness crept into her soul. "I'll be okay once I'm back at work tomorrow morning. Too much vacation isn't good—especially when you return home with nothing but an ache in your heart."

Sheila wasn't sure if the pain she felt was from not finding Grandma's doll or from missing Dwaine. Probably a little of both, she decided.

"This feeling of gloom will pass. All I need to do is keep busy." She headed for the kitchen. "I'll start by cleaning the refrigerator, and then I'll go to the store and buy something good to eat. Work and food—that's what I need right now."

The next few weeks went by in a blur as Sheila immersed herself in work and tried to forget she had ever met a man named Dwaine Woods. She'd had several more e-mails from him, but he never mentioned the doll. Sheila figured either he'd had no more leads or he had no interest in trying to find the Bye-Lo for her.

"It's just as well," Sheila muttered as she turned off her work computer on Tuesday afternoon and prepared to go home.

"Were you talking to me?" Dr. Taylor asked as he passed her desk.

Sheila felt heat creep up the back of her neck and spread quickly to her cheeks. She hadn't realized anyone else was in the room. She thought the doctor had gone home for the day.

"I didn't know you were still here."

He chuckled and pulled his fingers through the thinning gray hair at the back of his head. "If you weren't talking to me, who then?"

She stared at the blank computer screen. "Myself."

"I see. And did you have a suitable answer to your question?"

She shook her head. "I'm afraid there is no answer."

He snapped his fingers. "Sounds like a matter of the heart."

"It is," she admitted.

"Want to talk about it?"

It was tempting, for Dr. Taylor was not only an excellent chiropractor, but also a good listener, full of sound advice and godly counsel.

"It's nothing. I'll be fine," she murmured.

"All right then. I won't press the matter, but I will be praying for you."

"Thanks. I appreciate that."

"See you tomorrow morning." Dr. Taylor grabbed his briefcase from under the front counter and headed out the door.

Sheila picked up her purse and followed.

Dwaine had closed his shop for the day, deciding to clean out the drawers of an old rolltop desk he'd discovered in a shed out behind his shop.

He gulped down the last of his coffee and pulled open the first drawer. Inside were a bunch of rubber bands, some paper clips, and a small notebook. He thumbed through the pages to be sure there was nothing important, but halted when he came to the last page.

DOLL HOSPITAL—SEATTLE was scrawled in bold letters.

"That's odd. I wonder if Bill Summers took some old dolls there to be repaired."

Dwaine thought about the box of dolls he'd acquired several weeks before. He'd been planning to take them to Seattle during Easter vacation.

"I need to get those out, because I'll be leaving for Seattle next week," Dwaine muttered as he ripped the piece of paper with the bold writing from the notebook. "Don't have a clue what this is all about, but I sure am glad for the reminder that I need to take the dolls in for repair."

He shook his head. "I think Sheila was right about me being forgetful."

Dwaine closed the drawer and stood. He hadn't heard from Sheila in a couple of days and decided to check his e-mail.

A few minutes later, he was online. There was a message from his sister, Eileen, saying they were looking forward to seeing him. There were a few e-mails from other antique shops, but nothing from Sheila. Was she too busy to write, or had she forgotten about him already?

As soon as he clicked the icon to get off-line, he closed his eyes in prayer. "Father, I miss Sheila, and I really need Your help. If You want us to be together, please show me what to do."

He opened his eyes and glanced around the antique shop.

Sheila had done so much to make the place look better when she was here. "I think I'd better give her a call when I get back from Seattle."

Sheila had decided a few days ago that she probably wasn't going to hear from Dwaine again. It had been over a week since she'd received an e-mail from him.

"Maybe he's given up on me because all I ever ask about is Grandma's doll and I've never said how much I miss him." She shut the computer down and pushed away from her desk. "It's probably for the best. He needs to find someone who lives there in Casper, and I need to. . ." What did she need? Sheila headed for the kitchen. "I need to fix supper and get my mind off Dwaine and the doll he's never going to find."

She chuckled in spite of her melancholy mood. She was calling dinner "supper" now. She'd been converted to Casper, Wyoming's way of saying things. Or was it Dwaine's ways she'd been converted to? Had he gotten under her skin more than she realized—carved a place in her heart she could never forget?

Sheila spotted the black Bible with worn edges—the one Dwaine had found on Grandma's old piano. Grandma had told Sheila it belonged to Grandpa and said she'd like for Sheila to have it. At the time, Sheila had thought Grandma was trying to make up for the missing doll, but now, as she stared at the cover, she was filled with a strong desire to read God's Word. She'd forgotten to do devotions that morning and knew her day would have gone better if she had done them.

She sagged into a chair and breathed a prayer. "Lord, please speak to me through Your Word, and give me a sense of peace about the things that have been troubling me since I returned home."

She opened the Bible to the book of 1 Timothy. Her gaze came to rest on chapter 6, verses 7 and 8. *"For we brought nothing into the world, and we can take nothing out of it. But if we have food and clothing, we will be content with that."*

Tears welled up in her eyes. "Father, forgive me for putting so much emphasis on worldly things. You've obviously decided I don't need Grandma's doll, and I'm realizing how wrong I've been for concentrating on a worldly possession. I should be more concerned about my relationship with You, as well as friends and family. Help me to care more, love more, and do more to further Your kingdom. Amen."

The doorbell rang, and she jumped. "It's probably the paperboy, wanting to be paid for this month's subscription."

She padded down the hall to the front door and peered through the peephole. No one was there. At least, she couldn't see anyone.

Cautiously, Sheila opened the door. Nobody was on the porch, but a small cardboard box sat on the doormat. A yellow rose lay across the top of it.

She bent down and picked them both up.

"Sure hope you like roses."

Sheila bolted upright at the sound of a deep male voice. A voice she recognized and had longed to hear. "Dwaine?"

186

He peeked around the corner of the house and grinned at her.

"Wh–what are you doing here?" she rasped.

"Came to see you."

"What about the rose and package? What are they for?"

He stepped onto the porch. "The rose is to say, 'I've missed you,' and what's in the box is a gift from my heart."

She looked at the package, at Dwaine, and back at the package again. "What's in there?"

"Open it and find out."

Sheila handed him the rose and lifted the lid. She gasped, and her eyes clouded with tears as a Bye-Lo baby came into view. The skin on her arms turned to gooseflesh. Could it possibly be Grandma's old doll?

With trembling fingers and a galloping heart, Sheila raised the cotton nightgown. It was there—her name scrawled in black ink on the cloth stomach.

She clutched the Bye-Lo baby to her chest. "Oh Dwaine, where did you find her?"

"In Seattle. It's an interesting story. Can I step inside out of this heat?" Dwaine wiped the perspiration from his forehead.

"Yes, of course. Come in and I'll pour you some iced tea."

When they were both seated at the kitchen table with glasses of cold tea, Sheila said, "Don't keep me in suspense. Please tell me how all this came about."

Dwaine set down his glass and grinned. "It was an answer to prayer."

"Going to Seattle, finding the doll, or coming here?"

"All three." He leaned closer and she shivered, even though she wasn't cold.

His lips were inches from hers, and she could feel his warm breath against her face. Mustering all her willpower, Sheila leaned away. "H–how much do I owe you for the doll?"

"What?" Dwaine looked dazed.

"Bye-Lo. How much did she cost?"

"Nothing."

"Nothing?"

He shook his head. "Let me explain."

"Please do."

"Last week I was cleaning out an old desk I had found in the shed behind my shop, and I came across a notebook. One of the pages had the words 'Doll Hospital—Seattle,' written on it."

"That's all?"

"Yep. I had no idea what it meant, but it reminded me that I had a box of old dolls I wanted to take there." Dwaine paused to take another sip of tea. "After spending Easter with my sister and her family in Seattle, I went to the doll hospital the following day."

"That's where you found my grandmother's doll?"

He nodded. "As soon as I told the lady where I was from and that I was the new owner of The Older the Better Antique Shop, she lit right up. Said a Bye-Lo doll had been sent from the previous owner several months ago and that she'd never heard back from him."

"I'm surprised she didn't call the store."

"She said she'd tried but was told the number had been disconnected. Turns out she'd been given a wrong number." Dwaine set his glass back on the table. "Since she knew the number she'd called wasn't in service, she assumed the business had closed."

"So she kept the doll?"

"Right. She put in new eyes, since that's what it had been sent there for, and placed the doll in her display cabinet. Said she didn't want to sell the Bye-Lo in case the man who sent it ever tried to contact her."

Sheila stared at the doll lying on the table. Its pale pink bisque face looked as sweet as it had when she was a child. "You didn't have to buy it, then?"

"Nope. Just paid the woman the bill to fix the eyes."

"But what about the amount my grandmother was paid by the previous owner of your shop?"

Dwaine shrugged. "Don't know how much that was since I can't find a receipt."

"I'm sure Grandma knows what she sold it for."

He shook his head. "I called and asked, but she said she forgot."

"At least let me pay for the cost of the doll's repairs and your plane ticket to bring it to me." Sheila smiled. "You could have saved yourself the trouble and mailed it, you know."

He squinted and shook his head. "And miss the chance to see you?"

She squirmed in her chair as his expression grew more intense.

"I've missed you, Sheila. Missed your laughing eyes, beautiful smile, and even your organizational skills." He leaned closer. "I believe I've fallen in love with you."

Her mouth went dry. "You—you have?"

He nodded and lifted her chin with his thumb. "I know we haven't known each other very long, but when God brings a good thing into my life, I'd be a fool to ignore it."

"I agree."

His eyes twinkled. "You think I'm a good thing?"

"Oh yes," she murmured. "God's been showing me some important verses from His Word, and as happy as I am to have the precious Bye-Lo baby, I'm even more excited to see you."

As Dwaine's lips sought hers, Sheila felt like she was floating on a cloud. When the kiss ended, they both spoke at once.

"Does Fresno need another antique shop?"

"Does Casper need another chiropractor's receptionist?"

They laughed.

"I could use a secretary. As you already know, my shop was a mess before you came along." Dwaine took hold of her hand and gave it a gentle squeeze. "And I've been a mess since you left town."

"Me, too." Sheila smiled through her tears. "I've been doing a lot of thinking lately, and I've decided there's really nothing keeping me here in Fresno. I know, too, that building a relationship with someone as wonderful as you is far more important than my job or the old doll I used to play with as a child."

"You mean it?" He sounded hopeful, and his eyes searched her face. "What about your parents' house? Would you sell this place if you moved to Casper?"

She shook her head. "Just a minor detail. The house can be put up for rent."

His lips touched her forehead in a kiss as gentle as the flicker of butterfly wings. "I know it's probably too soon for a marriage proposal, but if you move to Casper, we can work on that."

She fingered the cloth body on the Bye-Lo baby. "And to think none of this would have happened if I hadn't come to Wyoming in search of Grandma's doll."

MATCHMAKER 911

DEDICATION

To my daughter-in-law, Jean,
whose first career was barbering.

CHAPTER 1

"Ya know what?" croaked an aged, gravelly-sounding voice. "I was six months old before I even saw the light of day!"

In the past four years of cutting customers' hair, Wendy Campbell had listened to more ridiculous jokes and boring stories than she cared to admit. Clyde Baxter sat in her antique barber's chair, and she was quite certain she was about to hear another joke or two from him. Barbering was her chosen profession, and as long as it wasn't an off-color joke, she would play along.

"Why's that, Clyde?" Wendy prompted, knowing if she didn't make some kind of response, the elderly man would probably tell her anyway.

"Well, darlin', my mother, God rest her soul, was a bit near-sighted. So the poor woman kept on diaperin' the wrong end!"

Wendy's muffled groan did nothing to deter the amicable man, and with no further encouragement, he continued. "Now, I don't want to say I was an ugly baby or anything, but I hear tell that the doctor who brought me into this ol' world took one look at my homely mug and promptly made a citizen's arrest on my daddy!" At this remark, Clyde roared with laughter.

Wendy grimaced. The joke was respectable enough, but thanks to Clyde's interruptions by moving around each time he laughed, this haircut was taking much longer than it should. It was only ten o'clock, and she still had several more clients scheduled in the next two hours—including four-year-old Benny Jensen, the kid who hated haircuts and liked to kick and scream. That didn't take into account any walk-ins who might happen by either.

Wendy could hardly wait for lunchtime when she could run home, grab a quick bite to eat, and check up on her father. At least *Dad* had sense enough not to tell a bunch of lame wisecracks and off-color stories. Wendy didn't mind cutting hair, and now that Dad couldn't work, she certainly needed the money. There were days like today though, when she wondered if a woman working in a predominately man's world was really such a good idea.

"Why, I'll never forget the day I graduated from grammar school," Clyde continued, with a silly grin plastered on his seventy-year-old, weathered face. "I tell you, I was so nervous I could hardly shave!" The old man laughed so hard this time that his whole body shook, and he had tears running down his wrinkled cheeks.

Wendy rolled her eyes toward the plastered ceiling and feigned a smile. "You'd better quit laughing and hold still, Clyde. If you don't, it might be your ear that comes off and not those sideburns you've finally decided to part with."

Clyde slapped his knee and let out another loud guffaw, ending it on a definite pig snort. "Tell ya what, honey, you could probably take my ear clean off, and it wouldn't make much never mind to me. I can only hear outa one ear anyways, and I ain't rightly sure which one that is!"

Without making any reply, Wendy took a few more snips and followed them with a quick once-over on the back of Clyde's stubbly neck with her clippers. She dusted him off with a soft-bristled brush and announced, "There you go, Clyde. That ought to hold you for at least another month."

Wendy was already moving toward her antiquated cash register, which had to be manually opened by the use of a handle on one side. Due to the hour, she sincerely hoped her joke-telling client would take the hint and move on.

Clyde finally stood up and ambled slowly over to where she stood, smiling through clenched teeth and waiting impatiently for him to pay. "You sure ain't much for fun today, are you, little lady?"

Before Wendy could think of an intelligent reply, Clyde added, "Nothin' like your old man, that's for sure. Why, good old Wayne used to tease like crazy all of the time. He could tell some jokes that just kept ya in stitches, too!"

Clyde appeared thoughtful, with a faraway look clouding his aging eyes. "I sure do miss that guy. It's been two years now since he took a razor to my chin or shortened my ears a few inches with them clippers of his. Such a downright shame that your daddy can't cut hair no more."

Wendy nodded, causing her short, blond curls to bounce. "Dad's been battling arthritis a long time. After two knee replacements and even having the joints in his fingers surgically repaired, I'm afraid the disease has finally gotten the best of him. He hardly gets out of the house anymore, unless it's to go to the hospital for his regular physical therapy appointments. Once in a while, he still stops by here, if the weather is good enough and he's not in too much pain. He likes to sit right there and reminisce." She pointed with the tip of her scissors to her dad's old barbering chair in the corner of her early American shop and swallowed the impulse to shed a few tears.

Clyde clicked his tongue noisily. "Wayne sure could cut hair."

Wendy brushed some of Clyde's prickly gray hair off the front of her blue cotton smock. "Yes, he was a great partner. Even when all Dad could do was sit and give me instructions, he taught me a whole lot that I never learned in barber's school."

The old man gave Wendy a quick wink. "Don't get me wrong, little lady. I wasn't tryin' to say you can't cut hair. For a little whip of a gal, you're a real whiz at scissor snippin'."

"Thanks—I think," Wendy said with a grin as Clyde handed her eight dollars for his haircut. She pulled sharply on the handle of the cash register, dropped the bills inside, then snapped the drawer shut. Wendy moved toward the front

door, assuming Clyde would follow.

"You know what a little gal like yourself really needs?" Clyde asked, obviously not in much of a hurry to leave.

Wendy drew in a deep breath then let it out in a rush. "No, Clyde, what *do* I need?"

Playfully, the old man poked her on the arm and laughed. "You need a man in your life—that's what you need. Maybe someone like that good-looking fellow Gabe Hunter."

Wendy bit down firmly on her bottom lip. She was trying so hard to be patient with Clyde, but if he didn't head for home soon, there was a good chance she might say something she would probably regret. Clyde didn't understand what it was like for her. No one did, really. She had a deep hurt from the past that affected her response to men. Having so many guys at the shop trying to make a play for her only made things worse.

"Dad is the only man I need," she affirmed, opening the front door and letting in a blast of chilly air. "I have all I can do just to take care of him and keep this little barbershop running."

Clyde shrugged and slipped into the heavy jacket he'd hung on one of the wooden wall pegs near the door. "Suit yourself, girlie, but I think a little romance might be just the ticket."

With that, he crammed his hands into his pockets and strolled out of the shop.

After Wendy swept the floor clean of hair one more time and

said good-bye to her final customer of the morning, she leaned heavily against the door and let out a low moan. Her stomach rumbled with hunger, and a feeling of weariness settled over her like a heavy blanket of fog. She licked her lips in anticipation of going home, where she could have something to eat, prop her feet up for a while, and get in a short visit with the only man in her life. Dad always seemed so eager to hear what was going on at the barbershop, often plying her with questions about who came in today, what they said or did, and whether Wendy was sure she could handle things on her own. Her father seemed to pride himself on being in total control. He'd run a barbershop for more than twenty years and sent her to barber's school so she could be his partner in this small Northwest town.

However, there were at least two things Wendy knew he hadn't been able to control. First, he'd had no control over his wife's untimely death, when she was killed by a drunk driver nearly ten years ago. That terrible accident had left him a widower with a young daughter to care for. Yet in all these years, she'd never heard him complain. Nor had her fifty-year-old father been able to control the doctor's diagnosis of severe rheumatoid arthritis many years ago. Wendy knew it had been a terrible blow, especially when he'd tried so hard to keep on working. Eventually, he had to turn the shop over to her and retire his barbering shears.

"Why did it have to happen? Sometimes life seems so unfair," Wendy lamented as she reached for her coat. As she closed the door, a chilling wind blew against Wendy's face,

stinging her eyes and causing her nose to run. "I'll be so glad when spring finally comes," she murmured. "At least then Dad will feel more like getting out."

Wendy's house was just a block from Campbell's Barbershop, so she always walked to and from work. The exercise did her good, and it only took a few minutes to get there. As usual, Wendy found the front door of their modest, brick-faced home unlocked. In a town as small as Plumers, everyone knew each other. The crime rate was almost nonexistent. Leaving doors and windows unlocked was one of the fringe benefits of small-town living.

Dad sat in his vibrating, heat-activated recliner, staring out the living room window. He offered Wendy a warm smile when she came though the door. Tipping his head, the dark hair now thinning and streaked with gray, he asked the proverbial question. "How's business?"

"About the same as usual, Dad," Wendy answered. "How was your morning?"

"About the same as usual." He chuckled. "Except for one thing."

She draped her coat over the back of the couch and took a seat. "Oh, and what was that?"

"Clyde Baxter phoned. We had quite a talk."

Wendy leaned her head back against the cushions. "Clyde was in the shop this morning. Of course, I'm sure he told you."

He lifted himself from the recliner and reached for his walking cane. "Clyde didn't tell any of his off-color jokes, I hope. I'll have a talk with him about that, if it's still a problem."

Wendy shook her head. "He was a perfect gentleman today. Just told a few clean jokes." She propped her feet on the coffee table and sighed deeply, choosing not to mention the fact that the elderly man's stories were repeats from other times he'd been in the shop. "So what else did Clyde have to say to you, Dad?"

"He thinks you need a man in your life," he said, grunting as he sat down beside her.

Wendy gritted her teeth. "Clyde doesn't know what he's talking about."

Dad reached out to lay a gnarled hand on her jean-clad knee. "You do spend most of your time running the barbershop and taking care of me. A young woman needs a social life. She needs—"

"You're all I need, Dad," Wendy interrupted. She gave his hand a few gentle pats, then abruptly stood. "I don't know about you, but I'm starving. What would you like for lunch?"

He shrugged. "I'm not all that hungry. I thought we could talk awhile."

"If it's about me finding a man, you can forget it." Wendy started for the kitchen but turned back just before she reached the adjoining door. "Dad, I know you have another physical therapy appointment this afternoon. Would you like me to close the shop and drive you over to the hospital in Grangely?"

Dad shook his head. "I've already called People for People, and they're sending a van out around one thirty."

Wendy nodded. "Okay, if that's what you want." She closed her eyes and inhaled sharply. At least she had managed

to successfully change the subject. She headed for the kitchen, wondering, *Now why does everyone suddenly think I need a man?*

Paramedic Kyle Rogers and his partner, Steve, had just brought an elderly woman to the hospital. She'd been doing some laundry and slipped going down the basement steps. The physicians determined a possible broken hip. Kyle left the woman in the emergency room and was heading to the cafeteria. Steve was parking their vehicle and planned to join him for a much-needed lunch after he checked their supplies.

I sure hope we don't get any more calls for a while, Kyle thought. *It's only three o'clock, but I'm completely beat!* The morning hours had been full, with several 911 calls coming from the three smaller towns surrounding Grangely. This afternoon they'd already had two local emergencies. Kyle would be the first to admit that the life of a paramedic was often grueling. A few good men and women burned out even before they reached their midthirties. Some became harsh and callous from witnessing so many maladies, too.

One of the worst tragedies Kyle had ever seen was a young college student who'd committed suicide by jumping out his dorm room window. The mere image of the distorted man made him cringe. Kyle knew he would never be able to handle such abhorrent things without Christ supporting him.

As he entered the cafeteria, Kyle saw a middle-aged man using a cane with one hand, trying to balance a tray filled with a cup of coffee and a donut with the other. It looked as if the poor fellow was about to lose the whole thing, as it tipped precariously this way and that. Before Kyle could respond, the cup tilted slightly, spilling some of the hot coffee onto the tray.

"Here, let me help you," he said to the red-faced man. "Where do you plan to sit? I'll set the tray on the table."

The man nodded toward the closest table. "Right there's fine."

Kyle put the tray down and pulled out a chair. "Here you go, sir."

The man's hand trembled as he reached it toward Kyle. "The name's Wayne Campbell, and I sure do appreciate your help, young man."

Kyle smiled warmly, and being careful not to apply too much pressure, he shook the arthritic hand briefly. "I'm Kyle Rogers, and I'm just glad I happened to be in the right place at the right time." Unconsciously, he reached up to place one finger against the small *WWJD* button he wore on his shirt pocket. Just thinking about the man's gnarled hands filled him with compassion. *I bet those hands used to be hardworking. Probably cradled a baby at one time, or maybe stroked a wife's cheeks with ease. The poor man has lost so much normal function that he couldn't even balance a tray with one hand.*

"Are all paramedics this helpful?" Wayne questioned, breaking into Kyle's thoughts.

Kyle shrugged and ran his fingers through his thick dark hair. "I can't speak for all paramedics, but I try to do whatever God asks of me."

Wayne nodded and took the offered seat. "You're welcome

to join me. In fact, I'd appreciate the company."

Kyle nodded. "Sure, why not? My partner's meeting me here for a late lunch, so if you don't mind sitting with a couple of tired paramedics, we'd be happy to share your table."

Wayne smiled in response. "No problem a'tall. I just finished with physical therapy and was planning to gulp down a cup of coffee and inhale a fattening donut before I head for home."

"I guess I'll go get myself a sandwich," Kyle said. "How about if I get you another cup of coffee?"

Wayne reached into his jacket pocket to retrieve his wallet. "Here, let me give you some money, then."

Kyle waved the gesture aside. "Don't worry about it." He grinned and moved over to the snack bar before the older man had a chance to respond.

A short time later, Kyle joined Wayne at the table, carrying a tray with one jelly donut, two cups of coffee, and a turkey club sandwich.

"You said this was your lunch?" Wayne asked as Kyle took a seat at the small table.

Kyle nodded. "We've been busy all day. There was no time to stop and eat at noon."

He bowed his head and offered a silent prayer of thanks for the food. When he opened his eyes and started to take a bite of sandwich, he noticed the arthritic man looking at him curiously.

"You rescue guys sure do keep long hours, don't you?" Wayne asked, slowly reaching for his cup of coffee.

"Sometimes our days can go anywhere from eight to twenty-four hours," Kyle admitted.

"Wow! That must be pretty hard on your family life."

Kyle shrugged. "I'm single, and it's probably a good thing, too. I don't have to worry about unpredictable hours causing my wife to burn dinner."

With a trembling hand, Wayne set the coffee cup down, spilling some as he did so. Kyle reached across the table and mopped up the mess with a few napkins.

Wayne frowned deeply. "Not only do I manage to nearly dump my whole tray, but I can't even drink a cup of coffee without spilling it all over the place." He shook his head and grumbled, "It's not bad enough that I've messed up my own life, but I'm afraid my only daughter will be strapped with me till the day I die."

Kyle glanced toward the cafeteria door. *Still no Steve. He must have gotten sidetracked along the way. Probably ran into one of those cute little nurses he likes to flirt with. Well, Lord, maybe my mission for the moment is to let this poor man unload some of his woes.* He gave Wayne Campbell his full attention. "What makes you think your daughter will be strapped with you?"

Wayne bit down on his bottom lip. "I'm a widower. My daughter, Wendy, not only works full-time, but has had the added burden of taking care of me for the last few years."

Kyle rubbed his forehead, praying for the right words of encouragement. "Does she complain about her situation?"

Wayne shrugged. "Not in so many words, but no matter

how brave a front she puts on, I can tell she's unhappy." He bumped his hand against the edge of the table and winced. "Her attitude at home is fine, but at work—well, the last time I observed things, she seemed kind of testy."

Kyle patted Wayne's arm gently. "Maybe all your daughter needs is more love and understanding."

Wayne nodded. "You know, you might be right about that, son. I think Wendy could use a little bit of romance."

CHAPTER 2

Today was Tuesday, the first day of Wendy's workweek. She'd just closed up shop for lunch and was heading down the street toward home when the piercing whine of a siren blared through the air. It was all Wendy could do to keep from covering her ears and screaming. Sirens reminded her of that fateful day when her mother was killed. Clare Campbell had always been a crusader, and keeping the roadside free of litter was one of her many campaigns. She'd been walking just outside of town, picking up garbage as she went.

Wendy, only fifteen at the time, had been at the barbershop that Saturday morning, flirting with all the teenage boys who'd come in for a haircut and watching her father work. She heard the eerie sirens as they whizzed through Plumers, wondering what had happened. Sirens in their small town

usually signaled some kind of serious mishap. A fire truck was sent from nearby Grangely for fires, and the paramedic vehicle came for accidents and serious ailments.

Wendy could still see the shocked expression on her dad's face when a police officer arrived at the barbershop and gave him the news that Mom had been hit by a car. Those sirens had been for her, only it was too little, too late. Clare Campbell was dead—killed instantly by a drunken driver who'd veered off the road.

The blaring sound drew closer now, pulling Wendy from the past and causing her to shiver. As the rescue vehicle flew past, she saw that it was the paramedic truck. Something serious must have happened. Someone would probably be taken to the hospital in Grangely.

Wendy began to walk a bit faster, broke into a cold sweat, then ran at full speed when she saw the vehicle stop in front of her house. It couldn't be! "Please, God, don't let anything happen to Dad," she prayed.

Two paramedics were already on the front porch when Wendy bounded up the stairs.

"It's open," she cried. "My father never locks the front door."

One of the men turned to face her. "Did you make the call?"

Wendy shook her head. "No, I just got here." She yanked open the front door and dashed into the living room.

Her father sat slumped over on the floor. His cane, one leg, and both hands were badly tangled in a long piece of fishing line. A well-used rod and reel were connected to the other end of the line, lying at an odd angle against the front of the couch. The phone was on the floor by his hip. Its cord was wrapped around the twisted mess.

"Dad, what on earth happened?" Wendy dropped to her knees beside him, and the paramedics moved swiftly toward their patient.

"Mr. Campbell?" Kyle Rogers could hardly believe it. This was the same man he'd spoken to in the hospital cafeteria just last week.

"You remember me?" Wayne inquired as Kyle donned a pair of surgical gloves.

"Of course. We met at the Grangely Hospital last week," Kyle replied. "You seem to have a bit of a problem, sir. Are you hurt? You didn't get a fishhook stuck in your hand or anything, did you?"

Wayne groaned and shook his head. "I don't think so, but I'm so glad you're here. I was trying to tie some flies, but I sure made a mess of things, didn't I?" He glanced over at Wendy, who was white faced and wide eyed. "Don't look so serious, Wendy girl. I met one of these young men at the hospital," he said, nodding toward Kyle. "He was nice enough to help me with some spilled coffee, and—"

"Dad, I'm concerned about you," Wendy interrupted. "How in the world did you get all tangled up like this?" Her forehead wrinkled. "And why didn't you call me instead of 911?"

Wayne shrugged. "Guess I thought you wouldn't know what to do." He glanced over at Kyle again. "Do you think you guys can get this stuff untangled? It's starting to cut off my circulation—what little I have left, that is," he added with a grimace.

Kyle turned to his partner. "Let's see what we can do to help the man, Steve."

As the two men began to work, Wayne smiled at his daughter and said, "Wendy, this is Kyle Rogers."

Kyle's full attention was focused on the job at hand as he tried to disengage the fishing line without causing Wayne too much discomfort. He did stop long enough to mumble, "Nice to meet you."

"Are you going to be able to get that line off Dad without breaking it?" Wendy asked, glancing at Kyle.

"That's what we're trying to find out, Miss Campbell," Steve answered. "If you'll just move aside so we can have more room to—"

"My daughter's name is Wendy," Wayne interrupted.

"I'm really sorry about all this," Wendy said apologetically. "I'm sure you busy men have better things to do than untangle a fishing line."

"That's okay, Wendy," Kyle said kindly. "We were free when the call came in, and this could have been a real emergency. What if that line had gotten tangled around your dad's neck?"

Wendy nodded and waited silently as Kyle and his partner tried unsuccessfully to unwind the line. Finally, when their efforts seemed futile, Steve took out a pair of scissors from his belt pouch and began to cut.

After a few minutes Kyle announced, "There you go, Mr. Campbell. Freedom at last!"

Wayne smiled as the paramedics helped him to his feet and onto the couch.

"Are you planning a fishing trip in the near future, Mr. Campbell?" Kyle asked as he moved aside the fishing pole that was still leaning against the couch.

"No—no—not really," Wayne sputtered. "I mean, maybe—"

Wendy gave her dad a quizzical look, but when he didn't acknowledge her, she turned to face Kyle. "If you think Dad's okay, then I'll excuse myself to go fix us some lunch. I need to get back to the barbershop by one."

"You're a barber?" Kyle asked, raising his eyebrows. *Wow! This really is a day full of surprises.*

She nodded. "I have been for the last five years."

"Wendy and I used to be partners," Wayne put in. "Then my rheumatoid arthritis got the best of me, and I finally had to hang up my shaving gear and retire the old scissors." He grunted. "Now I'm just a worthless, crippled widower who sits around wishing he could do something worthwhile with his life."

Steve was already moving toward the door, but Kyle wasn't in any hurry to leave just yet. He pulled out a chair from the dining room table and placed it directly in front of Wayne. He took a seat and leaned forward. "Look, Mr. Campbell, none of God's children are worthless. Just because you're a bit hampered by your arthritis doesn't mean you can't do

something worthwhile or have an active social life."

Wayne's eyes lit up. "You really think so?" He turned to Wendy. "Did you hear that? This nice young man thinks I have potential."

Wendy opened her mouth as if to comment, but was cut off when Steve held up the medication box and asked, "You about ready to head out, Kyle?"

Kyle waved one hand toward the front door. "You can wait for me in the truck. I'll just be a few more minutes."

Steve shrugged, grabbed the rest of their medical cases, and headed out the door.

"You know, Mr. Campbell—" Kyle began.

"Wayne. Please call me Wayne."

Kyle smiled and pointed toward the Bible lying on the coffee table. "I see you have a copy of the Good Book over there."

When Wayne nodded, Kyle continued. "I hope that means you put your faith in God."

"I try to, but I don't get to church much these days."

"My father doesn't drive the car anymore," Wendy explained.

Kyle eyed her with speculation. "What about you? Don't you drive?"

"Of course I do." She frowned. "Why do you ask?"

Before Kyle could respond, Wayne cut right in. "I bought Wendy a new car for her twenty-fourth birthday last month, and she makes a great chauffeur."

"Dad!" Wendy exclaimed. "I don't think Mr. Rogers cares

how old I am or that you just bought me a car."

Wayne shrugged and offered her an impish, teasing smile. "He did ask if you could drive."

Wendy drew in a deep breath and blew it out with such force, Kyle felt concern. "Are you all right, Miss Campbell?"

"I'm perfectly fine," she insisted. With a dimpled smile she added, "Thanks so much for rescuing Dad. I'm relieved there was no fishing hook involved and that it wasn't anything really serious. If you'll excuse me, I do need to fix lunch so I can get back to work."

Wendy started for the kitchen, but she stopped in her tracks when her father called, "Say, why don't we ask the paramedics to join us for lunch? You wouldn't mind fixing a little extra soup and some juicy roast beef sandwiches, would you, honey?"

Kyle glanced over at Wendy. She seemed a bit flustered, and he had a sudden desire to put her at ease. "I'm meeting someone for lunch, but thanks anyway," he said quickly.

Wendy's ears burned like a three-alarm fire. *What would possess Dad to invite someone for lunch without conferring with me first? It's just not like him to do something like that.* She shook her head, trying to make some sense out of this whole scene. One minute she had been frightened out of her wits by the sound of a siren, only to see the rescue truck stop in front of her house. The next moment, she was paralyzed with fear at the thought of her father being seriously hurt. Then she felt relief flood her soul when the paramedics were able to get Dad free

and discovered that he hadn't been injured in any way by the fishing line. Now Dad was inviting strangers to lunch! What was going on here, anyway?

"You take care, Mr. Campbell, and remember—God loves you," Kyle said, breaking into Wendy's disconcerting thoughts. "I'm sure if you pray about it, you can find something worthwhile to do." He smiled at Wendy. "It was nice meeting you."

Wendy's heartbeat picked up slightly, but she merely nodded and closed the door behind Kyle Rogers.

"Didn't you think those guys were great? Especially Kyle. What a nice young man he seems to be," her father said.

Wendy shrugged her shoulders. Kyle was nice, all right. And good-looking, too. His dark, wavy hair looked like something she would enjoy cutting, and those eyes—the color of her favorite chocolate candy. She shook her head, as if to knock some sense into it. She couldn't allow herself to think such thoughts. What had come over her, anyway?

"Paramedics are supposed to be good, Dad, or else they wouldn't be in the rescue business." Wendy flopped onto the couch. She grabbed a throw pillow and hugged it close to her chest. Her hands still trembled from the scare she'd just had, not to mention her unexplained attraction to one *very nice* paramedic. She felt a humdinger of a headache coming on, too. All thoughts of food suddenly faded.

"I know all about what paramedics are trained for," Dad said with a smile. "Allied Health Technical College in Grangely not only teaches emergency medical services but gives their students plenty of hands-on experience in the campus lab. The classroom training covers everything from cardiology basics to defensive driving of their emergency vehicles."

Wendy's mouth dropped open. "Just how in the world did you find out so much about paramedic training?" Before he could respond, she hurried on. "And why, Dad? Why would you need to know all that stuff?"

Dad smiled, causing his steel blue eyes to crinkle around the edges. "You know me. I'm always reading and doing some kind of research." He repositioned himself on the couch, then leaned his head against the cushions. "What else is there for a poor old cripple to do all day?"

Wendy shook her head. "You're only fifty, Dad. That's not old. And, while you're not filthy rich, you certainly aren't poor either. I make an adequate living at the barbershop, and your disability benefits help quite a bit."

He pointed a knobby finger at her. "You didn't bother touching on the subject of me being a cripple though, did you? That's because it's true."

Wendy began to knead her forehead. "Listen, Dad, I know being housebound so much of the time is probably getting to you, but you can't start feeling sorry for yourself. It won't solve a thing."

"Who says I'm feeling sorry for myself?" he snapped.

"Dad, I apologize."

"No, I'm the one who needs to do that," he said in a more subdued tone. "I don't know what came over me. I shouldn't have barked at you." He frowned and reached down to massage one leg. "Guess I'm in a bit of pain right now. It's making me

kind of touchy and out of sorts."

Wendy was immediately on her feet. "Oh Dad, I'm so sorry! How thoughtless of me to forget about the aspirin you usually take with your meal." She started toward the kitchen but turned back. "Listen, about lunch—"

"Just a bowl of soup will be fine for me," he interrupted. "Forget about the roast beef sandwich. I'm not all that hungry anyway."

She shook her head. "No, I wasn't going to ask that."

"What then?"

"I was wondering why you invited those paramedics to stay for lunch."

"They looked hungry," he replied with a Cheshire cat grin.

"Yeah, right," she countered. "You're such a kidder, Dad."

"I just thought it would be nice if we had some company for a change," Dad said, giving her a look that resembled a little-boy pout.

Wendy came back to kneel in front of the couch. "Dad, if you're really that bored, why not invite Fred or even good old Clyde over for lunch one of these days? If you give me some advance notice, I might even be willing to whip up something really nice."

He scowled. "Fred and Clyde? You've gotta be kidding, Wendy. Why, those guys and their same old jokes are boring."

"Dad!"

He smiled sheepishly. "Well, maybe not boring exactly, but certainly not full of vim and vigor, like those nice paramedics seemed to be."

Wendy groaned inwardly. She just didn't understand what had come over Dad. Maybe he was in his second childhood or something. Maybe he thought he needed to be around younger people in order to feel youthful.

She gave him a weak smile. "I *am* going out to the kitchen now. I think a bowl of chicken noodle soup might help both of our moods."

CHAPTER 3

"Oh brother," Wendy fumed as she closed the door behind what she hoped would be her last Friday morning customer. She needed at least half an hour to repair the damage left in the wake of little Jeffrey Peterson. Maybe by the time she'd eaten and checked on Dad, her emotions would have settled down.

"If the rest of my day goes as badly as the last few hours, I may consider closing this shop and finding a *normal* job!" she said, leaning against the edge of the counter.

First thing this morning, the Miller brothers came in—without appointments, of course. Rufus and Alvin lived in an old shack just outside of town, and the mere sight of the tall, gangly men made Wendy's stomach churn. Their clothes were always grimy and smelled like week-old dirty socks. The brothers' greasy, matted hair looked as if it hadn't been washed since their last cut, nearly eight weeks ago. It was a wonder they didn't have a head full of lice!

If that wasn't bad enough, both of the men sported the foulest breath she'd ever had the misfortune of smelling. To add insult to injury, Alvin spit his chewing tobacco into the potted palm sitting in one corner of the barbershop.

Jeffrey Peterson had been her next client, and what a time she'd had trying to get the active three-year-old to sit still! Even with the aide of the booster seat, he'd sat much too low. It was a miracle Wendy didn't take off an ear instead of the unruly mass of bright red hair, glued together by a hunk of bubble gum that could only be cut out. To make matters worse, Jeffrey managed to leave another wad of sticky gum on the arm of her barber's chair.

"Now wouldn't that give someone a nice bonus when they sit down, expecting a haircut or shave?" Wendy grumbled, scrubbing the gummy clump and wondering about the logic of buying that antique, claw-foot gum ball machine. "Maybe I should have gone to beauty school like my friend Sharon."

Suddenly the bell above her shop door rang, indicating another customer.

She looked up from her gum-removal project and scowled. It was Gabe Hunter, the very man old Clyde Baxter wanted to link her up with. *That will never happen,* Wendy fumed. *Gabe acts like a conceited creep, and the guy thinks he's every woman's dream come true.*

A quick glance at the wall clock told her it was eleven

thirty. While she certainly wasn't thrilled about this particular customer, she knew she could manage to squeeze in one more haircut before lunch.

"Morning, Wendy," Gabe said with a wink. "You're lookin' as pert and pretty as always."

"Flattery will get you nowhere, Gabe," Wendy said through clenched teeth. "At least not with me."

Gabe removed his leather jacket and carelessly threw it over one of the old opera-style seats in the small waiting room. "Aw, come on. You know you find me irresistible. I mean, how could you not? I'm probably your best-looking customer, not to mention the fact that I'm a great tipper." Gabe plopped into the chair Wendy had been scrubbing and planted his hairy hand inches from hers.

"Why don't you sit in that chair?" she suggested, pulling her hand away and motioning to what used to be her father's barber chair. "As you can probably see, this one has recently been initiated."

Gabe shrugged and moved to the other chair. "You know what?"

"No, what?" Wendy shot back.

"I don't have to start work until two today. How about you and me going over to Pete's Place and sharin' a large pepperoni pizza?"

"I'm working."

"Well, you've gotta take a lunch break, right?" he persisted.

Moving away from the gummed-up chair, Wendy grabbed a clean cotton drape and hooked it around Gabe's humongous neck. He'd been a star football player during high school, and now he worked as a mechanic for the only car repair shop in Plumers. Every time the brute came in for a haircut, he tried to come on to Wendy. Some of the town's young single women might be fooled by his good looks and somewhat crass charisma, but not Wendy. She'd been burned once, and she couldn't let it happen again. Especially not with some six-foot-two, blue-eyed charmer who didn't have the good sense to know when to keep his mouth shut.

"Well, how about it?"

"How about what?" Wendy sidestepped.

"Lunch—with me." He gave her another wink.

"I'm going home for lunch so I can check on Dad," she said evenly.

Gabe threw both hands in the hair, nearly pulling the cotton drape off his neck. "Whatever!"

"How much do you want off?" Wendy ignored his childish antics and made a firm attempt to get down to business. If she didn't get this guy out of the chair soon, not only would she be late for lunch, but what was left of her sanity would probably be long gone as well.

"Same as usual," came the casual reply. Then Gabe added with a wide grin, "You sure do have pretty blue eyes, Wendy Campbell."

Wendy closed those pretty eyes briefly and offered up a pleading entreaty. *Oh Lord, please give me strength.* It wasn't really much of a prayer, but it was the first one she'd petitioned God for since her father's 911 scare three days ago.

Wendy had accepted Christ as her Savior at an early age. She'd attended Sunday school and church for many years, too. Prayer and Bible reading used to be an important part of her life.

It wasn't until she began dating Dale Carlson while she was attending Bailey's Barber School in Spokane that things started to change. Dale had been the perfect Christian. . .or so he'd let on. Dale's mask of self-righteousness came catapulting off when he began making unwanted advances, asking Wendy to sacrifice her chastity. Not more than a week after putting Dale in his place, Wendy discovered he'd been seeing Michelle Stiles the whole time while coming on to her. The entire episode had shaken her faith in men and her own good judgment. Her relationship with Christ had suffered, as she was no longer sure she could even trust God.

"I don't think you're gonna get much hair taken off by just standin' there frowning like the world is about to end," Gabe declared, disrupting Wendy's reflections.

She shook her head, trying to reestablish her thoughts and get down to the business at hand. The sooner she got garish Gabe's curly black hair trimmed, the better it would be for both of them.

Half an hour later, Wendy had just taken the clippers to Gabe's neck and was about to dust him off when he announced, "That's not quite how I want it. Could you take a little more off the sides?"

Exasperated with this big hulk of a man, Wendy gritted her teeth, forcing herself as always to comply with the customer's wishes.

"I wouldn't mind having one of those neck rubs you're so famous for," Gabe said when the haircut was finished. "Yep, it sure would feel great to have your soft hands work some of the kinks out of my neck."

Right here is where I draw the line with this guy, Wendy reasoned silently. "I just don't have time for that today, Gabe," she said through tight lips. "I barely managed to squeeze you in for a haircut."

"You're sure not very sociable." Gabe stepped down from the chair. "I've spent the last half hour telling you how great we'd be together, and all you've done is give me the silent treatment."

Wendy chewed on her bottom lip, trying to hold back the words that threatened to roll off her tongue. She moved toward the cash register, hoping he would follow.

He did, but as soon as he handed her the money, Gabe blurted out, "If your mood doesn't improve some, you might start to lose customers." He shrugged into his black leather jacket. "Seriously, most folks don't come in here for just a shave or a good haircut, you know."

Wendy eyed him speculatively. "Oh? Why *do* they come in, Gabe?"

"A barber is kind of like a bartender," he said with another one of his irritating winks.

"Is that so?" Wendy could feel her temperature begin to rise, so she took a few deep breaths to keep from saying the wrong thing.

"Yep," Gabe retaliated. "Many barbershops—especially

ones that operate in small towns like Plumers—are noted as places where folks can share their problems, tell a few jokes, and let their hair down." He draped his muscular arm across her slender shoulders and smirked. "Get it, unfriendly Wendy? A good barber is supposed to be *friendly* and courteous to their customers."

Wendy grimaced. Gabe had stepped on her toes with that statement. She really did try to be polite to her customers, no matter how much they might irritate her. With Gabe, it was different. She didn't need men like him trying to put her down or take advantage. And she certainly wasn't going to give him the chance to make a complete fool of her the way Dale had.

"Have a nice day, Gabe," Wendy said in a strained voice.

He nodded curtly. "Sure. You, too."

The door was closing behind Gabe when Wendy heard it—that ear-piercing whine of a siren. She shuddered and glanced out the window. An emergency vehicle sped past the shop and headed up her street.

"Oh no," she moaned, "not again. Please, God, don't let it be going to my house this time."

Kyle Rogers couldn't believe he was being called back to the same house he'd been to only a few days ago. The dispatcher said Wayne had called asking for help because he was in terrible pain. What really seemed strange was the fact that the 911 call had come in about the same time as three days earlier. He shrugged. *Probably just a coincidence.*

"Ready?" Kyle asked Steve, opening the door of their truck and grabbing his rescue case.

"Ready," Steve said with a nod.

Kyle rapped on the front door. A distressed-sounding voice called out, "It's open. Come in."

When they stepped into the living room, they found Wayne lying on the couch.

"What is it, sir?" Kyle asked, kneeling on the floor in front of the couch. He had just put on his gloves when Wayne reached out to clasp his hand.

"I—I've got a cramp in my leg, and it's killing me! Wendy's not home from work yet, but she should be here soon." He drew his leg up and winced in pain as Kyle began probing.

"Is this where the cramp is, Mr. Campbell?"

Wayne shook his head. "No. I mean, yes—I think it's there."

"Do you get leg cramps very often?" Kyle inquired.

"Sometimes. It goes along with having rheumatoid arthritis, you know." Wayne glanced at the door. "Where is Wendy, anyway? She should be home by now."

Kyle gently massaged Wayne's contorted limb. "Is this helping any?"

Wayne thrashed about. "No, no, it still hurts like crazy. I think it's getting worse, not better!" He began moaning, then started gasping for breath. "I can't take it! I can't take any more!"

"Calm down, Mr. Campbell," Steve admonished. "You're only making it worse."

"He's hyperventilating, Steve. Get a bag."

Steve reached into their supply case and quickly followed instructions, placing a brown paper sack over Wayne's nose and mouth. "Do you think he could be having a panic attack, Kyle?"

Kyle nodded. "It looks that way. Once he begins to relax, we can work on that leg cramp."

The uncooperative patient pushed the bag aside. "Wendy—she—"

"I don't think we should be concerned about your daughter right now," Kyle asserted. "Let's get you calmed down; then we'll see if we can't take care of that charley horse." Kyle took the paper sack from Wayne and held it to his face again. "Breathe as normally as you can, and please, no more talking until we say."

A red-faced Wayne finally complied, settling back against the throw pillows.

Steve had just started to massage the leg again when Wendy came flying into the house.

"What happened? Is my dad sick? He wasn't playing with his fishing line again, I hope." Her eyes were huge as saucers, and her face white like chalk.

Kyle eyed her with concern. "Steady now, Miss Campbell. Why don't you have a seat?"

With an audible moan, Wendy dropped into the rocking chair. "Please tell me what's wrong with Dad."

"He called 911 because he was in terrible pain. When we got here, he said his leg had cramped up," Kyle explained.

"What's the paper sack for?"

"He started hyperventilating," Kyle replied.

"What would cause that?" She leaned forward with both hands on her knees.

"Probably a panic attack, brought on by the stress of not being able to get the pain stopped," Steve interjected.

Wayne was trying to remove the sack again, but Kyle shook his head. "Let's keep it there for a few more moments, Mr. Campbell. It will help you calm down; then you'll be able to breathe better." Kyle turned to Wendy. "Does your father get many severe leg cramps?"

She shrugged. "Some, but nothing he can't usually work out with a bit of massage or some heat." She looked at her father with obvious concern. "Dad, when did the cramping start, and why didn't you call me instead of 911?"

Kyle pulled the sack away so Wayne could respond to his daughter's question.

"I didn't want to bother you," Wayne mumbled.

"Wouldn't it have been better to interrupt my day than to make these men answer a call that could have been handled with a simple heating pad?"

Wayne tipped his head to one side and blinked rapidly. "Guess I didn't think about that. I just wanted to get some relief, and it hurt like crazy, so—"

"When was the last time you had some aspirin?" Steve asked.

"He has to take it with food, or it upsets his stomach," Wendy glanced over at her Dad with an anxious look. "I'd better fix some lunch so you can take your pills."

Wayne nodded and pulled himself to a sitting position.

"The leg cramp's gone now." He looked up at Wendy. "Some of that take-and-bake pizza you bought last night would sure be good."

"Okay, Dad, if that's what you want."

Wendy was almost to the kitchen when Wayne called, "Let's invite these nice young men to join us. How about it, guys? It's lunchtime. Does pizza sound good to you?"

"Sure does," Steve was quick to say.

"Count me in, too," Kyle agreed. He cast a quick glance at Wendy. "That is, if it's not too much trouble."

Wendy smiled. "No trouble at all."

Wendy sat across the table from her dad, watching with interest as he and the other two men interacted. *He really is lonesome,* she thought ruefully. *How could I have let this happen?* She began to massage her forehead. *I've got to figure out some way to help fill Dad's lonely hours.*

"Wendy, are you listening? Kyle asked you a question."

Wendy snapped to attention at the sound of Dad's deep voice. "What was it?" She looked at Kyle, who sat in the chair beside her.

"I was wondering about your barbershop."

"What about it?"

"What are your hours? Do you only take appointments?"

"I do take walk-ins, but many of my customers make appointments. The barbershop is open Tuesday through Saturday, from nine in the morning until five at night, with an hour off for lunch at noon." Wendy eyed him curiously. "Why do you ask?" Her heart fluttered as she awaited his answer. Was she actually hoping he might come in for a haircut?

Kyle shrugged. "Just wondering."

"How did you become a barber?" Steve asked. "Isn't that kind of unusual work for a woman?"

"Actually, I've heard that some of the finest barbers are women," Kyle inserted before Wendy could answer.

"That's right," agreed her father, "and my Wendy girl is one of them. Why, she graduated in the top five of her barbering class."

"Spoken like a proud papa," Kyle said with a grin.

"Dad tends to be a little bit prejudiced," Wendy was quick to say. "After all, I am his only daughter."

"And the only breadwinner these days," Dad added, bringing a note of regret into the conversation.

"I served my apprenticeship under Dad," Wendy said, hoping to dispel the gloomy look on Dad's face. "He sometimes forgets that I wasn't always so capable." She shook her head. "If you had time to listen, I'll bet he could tell you some real horror stories about how I messed up several people's hair during those early years. Dad is a wonderful, ever-patient teacher, and if I do anything well, I owe it all to him."

Steve laughed, but Kyle seemed to be deep in thought. Finally, he reached for another slice of pizza and took a bite. "Mmm. . .this is sure good." He washed it down with a gulp of iced tea, then changed the subject. "Say, Mr. Campbell, I know you were tying some flies the other day, and I was just

wondering if you've done much fishing lately. I hear there's some pretty good trout in several of the streams around here."

Dad rubbed his chin thoughtfully. "I used to fish a lot—back when I could still function on my own, that is."

"When was the last time you went fishing?" Kyle asked, leaning forward on his elbows.

"Well, let's see now," Dad began. "I guess it's been a little more than two years since my last fishing trip. My buddy Fred and I went up to Plumers Creek one spring morning. We sat on the grassy banks all day, just basking in the warm sun, shootin' the breeze, and reeling in some of the most gorgeous trout you'd ever want to see."

"Plumers Creek is a great place to fish," Steve put in. "I've been there a few times myself. How come you've never been back, sir?"

"I don't really think Dad's up to any fishing trips," Wendy interjected. "You saw the way his leg cramped up." She grimaced. "I'm sorry, but there are times when I have to wonder if all men ever think about is hunting, fishing, and telling contemptible jokes."

Three pairs of eyes focused on Wendy, and Dad's face had turned as red as the pizza sauce.

"I, uh, think maybe we'd better go," Steve said, sliding his chair away from the table. "The pizza was great. Thanks, Miss Campbell."

"No, no, you can't leave yet!" Dad protested. "I mean, we were just beginning to get acquainted."

"Our lunch hour's not quite over yet, so we can hang out a

few more minutes," Kyle said.

"I really do need to get back to work, Dad." Wendy stood up and grabbed the empty pizza pan. Not only was she going to be late for work if she didn't leave now, but she didn't care much for the direction this conversation was going. There was no point giving Dad false hope, and besides, sitting next to ever-smiling Kyle Rogers was making her nervous.

"Since your cramp is gone and you seem to be feeling better," Wendy said, moving across the room, "I'll leave you in the capable hands of these paramedics."

CHAPTER 4

Twice in one week! Wendy fretted. *Was it a coincidence that Dad called 911 so often, or did he really think it was an emergency? Was Dad merely "crying wolf" just to get some special attention?*

Wendy was glad they'd made it through the weekend without any more problems. Yesterday she scheduled a doctor's appointment for her dad; today, right after work, she'd be taking him in for an exam. He didn't know she'd done it though. He'd been so adamant about his leg feeling better and had assured her several times that there was no more cramping and no need to see Dr. Hastings until his regular checkup later in the month. She'd tell him about his appointment and try to make him see reason when she went home for lunch today.

Wendy's nerves felt all tied up in knots. Maybe that was why she'd been so testy the other day when the paramedics were talking to Dad about fishing. She didn't need any more chilling 911 calls to deal with either. What she really needed was a little peace and quiet. Maybe she should close the shop for a few days and stay home with Dad.

"That's probably not the best solution though," she murmured as she put the OPEN sign in the front door of the barbershop. "What I really need is to concentrate on finding some way to make him feel more useful and less lonely. If Dad won't take the initiative, then maybe *I* should give some of his buddies a call about lunch."

Wendy's first scheduled appointment wasn't until ten o'clock, so that gave her a whole hour. She drew in a deep breath and reached for the telephone.

After several rings, a gravelly voice came on the line. "Fred Hastings here. What can I do ya for?"

"Fred, this is Wendy Campbell, and I need to ask you a favor."

"Sure, ask away," Fred said with a deep chuckle.

"You and Dad are pretty good friends. Isn't that right?" Wendy drummed her fingers against the counter where the old rotary-dial phone sat.

"Yep. Right as rain. Why do ya ask?"

"When was the last time you paid Dad a visit?"

There was a long pause.

"Fred? Are you still there?"

"Yep, I'm still here. Let's see now. . . I think it was last month, when I dropped some fishin' magazines by your house."

Wendy grimaced. Fishing magazines? Those were the last

things Dad needed, since he could no longer fish. What was the point of adding fuel to the fire by reminding him of what he couldn't do? No wonder he was trying to tie fishing flies.

"Your dad and me went fishin' a few years ago, and—"

A low moan escaped Wendy's lips as Fred began a long, detailed narration of the last time he and her dad had gone up to Plumers Creek. She was trying to figure out the best way to politely get back to the reason for her call when the front door opened, jingling the bell and announcing an unscheduled customer. Wendy turned her head toward the door, and her mouth fell open. There stood Kyle Rogers, wearing a pair of blue jeans and a red flannel shirt. He looked so manly and rugged. Kind of like one of those lumberjacks who often came into the shop—only he was much better-looking. Another distinction was the fact that none of the woodsmen wore a religious pin on their shirt pocket, announcing to the world that they were trying to live and respond to others as Jesus would.

What would Jesus do right now? Wendy mused. She forced her thoughts back to the one-way phone conversation and cleared her throat loudly. "Um, Fred—someone just came into the shop. I'll have to call you back another time." She hung up and slowly moved toward Kyle.

He smiled softly and ran long fingers through his thick brown hair. "Hi, Wendy. Do you have time to squeeze me in?"

"Squeeze you in?" she squeaked.

"For a shave and a haircut." Kyle rubbed his stubbly chin and chuckled. "I've heard through the grapevine that you not only cut hair well but can give a really close shave."

Was Kyle flirting with her? Well, why wouldn't he be? Gabe did, and a few other guys seemed to think they could make a play for the town's lady barber, too. Why should Paramedic Rogers be any different? "I was trying to get some phone calls made, but I guess I could manage a shave and haircut," she said as politely as possible.

He started to move toward her, then stopped. "If this is going to be a problem, I could make an appointment and come back a little later. This is my day off, so—"

Wendy held up one hand. "No, that's okay. The rest of my day is pretty full, so it'll have to be now, I guess."

"Okay, thanks," Kyle said with a grin. "If I wait much longer for a haircut, I might get fired for looking like a bum."

Wendy reached for a cotton drape cloth and snapped it open, nodding toward her barber chair. "Have a seat."

Kyle quickly complied. When he was seated, with his head leaning against the headrest, Wendy hit the lever on the side of the chair, tipping it back so she could begin the shave.

"I'm sorry about the other day," Kyle said while she slapped a big glob of slick white shaving foam against one side of his face.

"Oh? What do you have to be sorry about?" she asked, keeping her tone strictly businesslike.

"For upsetting you." Kyle turned his head slightly so she could lather the other side as well. "You were upset when we started talking about fishing, right?"

Wendy shrugged. "Not upset, really. I just don't like it

when someone gives Dad false hope."

"False hope? Oh, you mean about going fishing?"

Wendy nodded curtly. "You'd better close your mouth now, or you might end up with it full of shaving cream."

Kyle could only nod at this point, because she'd just placed a pleasantly hot, wet towel over his entire face. He drew in a deep breath, closed his eyes, and allowed himself to relax. Wow! This felt like heaven. Too bad the cute little blond administering all this special attention didn't seem to care much for him. She seemed distant, and if his instincts were working as well as usual, Kyle guessed her father might be right. Maybe Wendy did feel strapped, having to care for him and run a barbershop by herself. He couldn't even begin to imagine what it must be like for her to give shaves and cut men's hair five days a week. From what he'd witnessed in other barbershops, some of the clientele could be pretty crass and rude at times.

Kyle's forehead wrinkled. *I wonder if either Wendy or Wayne ever does anything just for fun. Maybe what they need is something positive to focus on. With God's help, maybe I can figure out some way to help them both.*

Wendy let Kyle sit with the warm towel on his face for several minutes, knowing that the procedure would not only cleanse the face, but also soften his bristly whiskers. When she lifted it off, he opened his mouth as if he had to say something, but she quickly wiped his face clean and applied more shaving cream.

"Phase two," she explained at his questioning look.

He nodded.

Wendy began to use the straight razor on her client's appealing face. She'd shaved a lot of handsome faces during her years as a barber, but none had ever evoked quite the response from her as Kyle Rogers. It was unnerving the way he looked at her—with dark, serious eyes and a smile that actually seemed sincere.

That's just it, Wendy groaned inwardly. *He "seems" sincere. . . but is he really? Probably not,* she silently acknowledged. *Except for Dad, I can't think of a single man who is truly sincere.* She drew in a deep breath, bringing all the pain of the past right along with it. *Dale wasn't sincere, that's for sure.*

"Are you okay?"

She blinked. "Huh? What do you mean?"

"You look like you're distressed about something."

Wendy gave her head a slight toss. "Sure, I'm fine." She hit the lever on the side of the chair, and it shot into a sitting position with such force, Kyle's head snapped forward. "Oh! I'm sorry about that," she said, reaching for a bottle of aftershave lotion on the shelf behind her. "This chair's a genuine antique, and sometimes when the levers are messed with, it seems to have a mind of its own."

Wendy patted the spicy liquid onto Kyle's freshly shaven face. He winced. "Do all your customers receive such treatment, or do you only reserve the rough stuff for guys like me?"

"Sorry," she said again. "Maybe your face is more sensitive than some."

"Guess so. That's what happens when you rely on an electric instead of a razor blade." He smiled up at her. "You sure have pretty blue eyes, do you know that?"

Oh no. . .here it comes, she fumed. *That lay-it-on-thick, make-a-move-on-Wendy routine.* She should have guessed Kyle was too good to be true. "How much hair do you want cut off?" she asked evenly.

He shook his wavy, dark mane. "Guess maybe you'd better take about an inch all the way around."

Wendy deftly began snipping here and there, never taking her eyes off the job at hand, trying to still the racing of her heart. Was she really dumb enough to be attracted to Kyle Rogers, or was her heart beating a staccato because she was irritated about his slick-talking ways and the silly, crooked grin he kept casting in her direction?

"Did you drive your dad to church on Sunday?" Kyle asked unexpectedly.

"No, I didn't. Why do you ask?"

"When I responded to Wayne's first 911 call, he made some mention of not getting out much," Kyle reminded her. "He said he can't drive to church anymore, so I was thinking maybe I could—"

"Well, don't worry about it," Wendy asserted. "If Dad wants a ride, he knows all he has to do is ask me."

"Do you go out much?"

"Huh?" Just where was this conversation leading? She

stopped her work and turned his chair so she could see both of their reflections in the antique beveled mirror. "Just so you know—I don't date—period."

He frowned. "Really? In your line of work, I thought you'd probably have a bunch of guys standing in line."

"I'm far too busy trying to keep this shop running," she said. "And as I'm sure you must have noticed, Dad needs my help at home."

"I realize that, Wendy, but you do have a life of your own, and—"

"No, actually, I don't!" She gave the chair a sharp turn so she could resume work.

"Then I suppose you wouldn't be interested in attending a Christian concert at my church in Grangely tonight?" Kyle asked.

Wendy clenched her jaw so hard she could feel a dull ache. Never had she wanted to finish a haircut so badly. What was it about Kyle that affected her so?

"I plan to spend the evening playing a few games with my dad," she informed him. "I think he's bored and needs me to spend more quality time with him."

"Maybe he needs to get out of the house more," Kyle suggested.

Wendy stopped cutting again and held the scissors directly over her client's head. "I appreciate your concerns, Kyle, but my father's needs are really *my* business."

He shrugged. "I just thought Wayne might like to go to that concert with us, that's all. There's a very special widow

who goes to my church, and since your dad said he likes to fish—"

"Fish?" She grimaced. "What's fishing got to do with a church concert?"

"Nothing," he admitted. "Maybe everything."

Wendy started cutting his hair again. "I don't follow you."

"Edna Stone—the widow I just mentioned—likes to fish," Kyle explained. "In fact, she goes fishing nearly every week. If we could get your dad and Edna to meet, they might strike up a friendship and maybe even go fishing together."

So it really wasn't a date he was asking her on after all. It was her dad he was trying to help. Wendy had obviously misjudged his intentions. However, that reality didn't make her feel much better. In fact, she wasn't sure how she was feeling about now.

"So what are you?" she asked. "Some kind of 911 match-maker?" Before Kyle could respond, she rushed on. "Really, the last thing Dad needs is some fisherwoman." She made a few more scissor snips, then added, "And need I remind you that he is disabled?"

"I know that, Wendy, but it doesn't mean he has to stop living."

"He's gotten along just fine for the last ten years without a wife, and I don't think he needs or even wants one now."

Kyle held up one hand. "I wasn't insinuating that Wayne and Edna would soon be walking down the aisle together." He grinned. "Of course, I suppose that could happen if the two of them should hit it off."

Wendy placed her scissors on the counter, then stepped in front of the barber chair. "I'm only going to say this once, and I hope you understand."

Kyle nodded. "I'm all ears."

Wendy blinked back threatening tears that had unexpectedly filled her eyes. "Dad doesn't need a woman friend or a wife. He just needs me to help fill his lonely hours." She inhaled sharply. "And I'm already working on that."

CHAPTER 5

As Kyle closed the door of his Bronco and started up the engine, he fought the urge to go back to Campbell's Barbershop. He dropped his head forward until it rested on the steering wheel. *Am I treading on thin ice, Lord?* he prayed. *Am I interested in Wayne and Wendy Campbell because I see a real need, or am I merely experiencing some kind of unexplained physical attraction to the cute little blond barber?*

Kyle didn't date much, mostly because of his crazy work schedule. However, if he were completely honest, he'd have to admit that he was concerned about establishing any kind of serious relationship that might lead to marriage. The life of a paramedic was far from ideal, and trying to balance his career with a wife and children would be difficult at best. He had no right to subject another human being to his "calling." He really should only date women he would never be apt to become romantically involved with.

"Wendy's father says he's a Christian, but I'm not so sure about Wendy," Kyle said, lifting his head from the steering wheel and turning the key in the ignition. She'd made no profession of Christianity and apparently didn't attend church. "She doesn't seem to have any interest in men or dating either," he murmured.

He pulled away from the curb with a slight smile tugging at the corners of his mouth. "Wayne Campbell needs some help, and I'm pretty sure Wendy does, too, Lord. So if I am the one to help them, I'm asking for Your guidance in all this."

Wendy was closing the barbershop at noon when she heard the distinctive whine of sirens in the distance. As the sound drew closer, she felt a funny feeling in the pit of her stomach. She uttered a quick prayer. "Not again, Lord. Please don't let it be another false alarm."

Wendy grabbed her coat. "What am I saying? Do I want a real emergency this time?"

She jerked the door open just in time to see the rescue vehicle fly past her shop. Stepping onto the sidewalk, Wendy could see clear up the street. She watched in horror as the truck came to a full stop in front of her house.

"Oh no!" she groaned. Not sure whether to be angry with her father or concerned for his welfare, Wendy made a mad dash for home. She stepped onto the porch just in time to

meet Steve and an older paramedic who identified himself as Phil Givens. "What's the problem?" she asked breathlessly.

Steve shook his head. "Not sure. When we received the call, the 911 operator said she could hardly make heads or tails out of the man's frantic plea for help."

This had better be for real this time, Wendy fussed inwardly. But even as the words flew into her mind, she reprimanded herself. If Dad really was sick, he needed help, and she needed to be with him. She threw open the front door and spotted her father, sitting in his recliner. He didn't look one bit sick. In fact, Wendy thought he looked more anxious than ill.

"Where's Kyle?" her father asked, looking past Wendy and the two rescue men who had followed her inside.

"Kyle has the day off, Mr. Campbell," Steve explained. "Phil always fills in for him on Tuesdays."

Before Dad could say anything more, both men had opened their rescue cases and donned their surgical gloves.

"What seems to be the problem?" Phil asked in a businesslike tone. "I understand your call was pretty vague."

"I—uh—was feeling kind of dizzy," he stammered. "I'm much better now though. Probably just got up too quickly."

"We're here, so we may as well check you out," Phil said with a curt nod.

"I agree," Steve put in. "It could be something serious this time."

Phil gave him an odd look. "What do you mean, *this* time?"

Steve shrugged. "This is the third call to this house in two weeks."

"And I just can't believe it," Wendy moaned. "What's the problem, Dad?"

He hung his head. "Nothing. I mean, I thought I was feeling kind of dizzy before, but now—"

"And now you're feeling just fine and dandy? Is that it?" Wendy lamented. She dropped to her knees in front of his chair. "Dad, do you know how bad you scared me?"

"We'll check him over in case there is something really wrong," Steve said before Dad could make any kind of reply.

Wendy turned to face the paramedic. "Just so you know, I have no pizza today."

Phil's expression revealed his obvious bewilderment. "Pizza? What's that supposed to mean?"

"Nothing. It doesn't mean anything at all," Dad cut in.

"Maybe what you need is a cat, Dad," Wendy muttered.

Dad looked at her as if she'd completely lost her mind. "I think you men had better go now," he mumbled. "My daughter and I have a few things to discuss."

Steve hesitated. "But you said you were feeling dizzy. Are you sure you're all right?"

"I'm fine, really." Dad struggled to sit up again. "Sorry about the wasted trip to Plumers."

"You really should think twice about calling 911," Phil said firmly. "We are extremely busy, and responding to unnecessary calls doesn't set very well with me."

Wendy gave the man an icy stare. "Dad *thought* he was sick."

Phil shot her a look of irritation in return, then nodded to

Steve. "Let's get going."

"A cat or dog might not be such a bad idea," Steve whispered as Wendy saw them out the door.

"It's either that, or I may have to consider moving Dad to the Grangely Fire and Rescue Station," Wendy said with a faint smile. She closed the door and leaned heavily against it, wondering what she was going to say to Dad, and how to say it without hurting his feelings.

"Look, Dad," she began, moving back to the living room, "I know you're probably lonely, and—"

He held up one hand as if to silence her. "I'm afraid I have an admission to make."

"Oh, and what might that be?" she asked with raised eyebrows.

"All three of my 911 calls were trumped up."

Wendy waved both hands in the air. "No? You think?"

He laughed lightly, but she didn't respond to his mirth. Those calls had frightened her, and she saw nothing funny about calling out the paramedics for false alarms either.

He motioned her to take a seat. "It's like this, honey—I thought Kyle Rogers would be working today, so—"

"Kyle has the day off," Wendy interrupted. "He came into the barbershop for a shave and a haircut this morning."

Dad's face brightened considerably. "He did?"

Wendy nodded. "Yes, but it might be the first and last cut he ever gets at Campbell's Barbershop."

"Oh, Wendy! You didn't scare him off, I hope."

"Scare him off? What's that supposed to mean, Dad?"

"Kyle's a nice young Christian man, and I think he would make good husband material."

Wendy moaned. "Husband material? Oh, Dad, please don't tell me you've been trying to set us up."

He shrugged, a smile playing at the corners of his mouth. "Okay, I won't tell you that."

"Dad! How could you?"

He hung his head sheepishly. "I thought you needed a man. I thought it might help—"

The rest of his sentence was lost on Wendy. All she could think of was the fact that everything had finally come into crystal-clear focus. Dad wasn't really that lonely after all. The old schemer was trying to set her up. What in the world was she going to do about this?

Right after lunch, Wendy convinced her dad to take a nap. He had seemed a bit overwrought ever since the paramedics left, and she thought he needed some rest. Besides, it would give her a chance to think things through more clearly.

Wendy closed the door to his bedroom and headed across the hall to her own room. She grabbed the telephone from the small table by her bed and dialed the Grangely Clinic. Since Dad was feeling fine, she saw no reason for him to see Dr. Hastings this afternoon after all.

A few minutes later, the appointment she'd scheduled had been canceled, and Wendy hung up the receiver. At least, she thought it was hung up. Preoccupied with thoughts of Kyle,

Dad, and her own self-doubts, Wendy missed fitting the receiver completely into the cradle. She left the room quickly and took a peek at Dad. He was sleeping like a baby, so she grabbed her coat and headed out the front door.

Outside the house, the air felt frigid. From the gray clouds gathering in the sky, it looked like it might even snow. Wendy stuffed her hands inside her pockets and hurried down the street toward her barbershop, hoping the storm wouldn't be too severe.

When she arrived at the shop, good old, joke-telling Clyde Baxter was waiting outside the door. He was leaning up against the building, just under the swirling, traditional candy-cane-style barber pole, blowing on his hands and stomping his feet up and down. "You're late," he grumbled, "and it's gettin' mighty cold out here. My eyes are sure smartin', too."

When Wendy apologized, his irritation seemed to vanish as quickly as it had come. He chuckled softly and said, "Say, here's a question for you, little lady. When are eyes not eyes?"

Wendy shrugged and opened the shop door. "Beats me."

"When the wind makes them water!" Clyde howled as he stepped inside, then slipped out of his heavy jacket and hung it on a wall peg.

Hanging up her own coat, Wendy let out a pathetic groan. "Sorry, Clyde, but I'm afraid I'm not in much of a laughing mood today. Things got a little confusing at home during lunch, and I ended up staying longer than usual."

"Everything okay with your dad?"

Wendy nodded. "Besides his arthritis, the only thing

wrong with Dad is a very bad case of meddleitis."

Clyde's bushy white eyebrows shot up. "What's that supposed to mean?"

She shrugged. "Never mind. You probably wouldn't understand anyway."

"Try me," Clyde said as he took a seat in Wendy's chair and leaned his head back in readiness for a shave.

Wendy drew in a deep breath and let it out in a rush. "For some reason, Dad thinks I need a man, and he's been making 911 calls in order to play matchmaker." She grabbed a handful of shaving cream and was about to apply it to Clyde's face when he stopped her.

"Whoa, hold on just a minute, little lady. I wholeheartedly agree with the part about your needin' a man, but what's all this about Wayne calling 911?"

Wendy bit her bottom lip so hard she tasted blood. Wincing, she replied, "In the past two weeks, he's called the Grangely Fire and Rescue Department three times, and they were all false alarms."

"Are you sure? I mean, maybe his arthritis is gettin' the best of him, and he just can't cut the mustard no more," Clyde defended.

Wendy shook her head, patting the shaving foam into place on the old man's weathered cheeks. "They were *planned* false alarms, believe me."

Clyde squinted. "Even if they were, what's that got to do with Wayne becomin' a matchmaker?"

"He's trying to pair me up with one of the paramedics

who's been responding to his fake calls," Wendy replied. "It took awhile to learn the truth, but now that I know just what Dad's little game is, I've got a few games up my own sleeve." She shot him a playful wink. "We'll just see who wins this war."

"I thought you said it was a game," Clyde mentioned as she dropped a hot towel over his face.

"It is," she said with a wry grin. "A war game!"

CHAPTER 6

Wendy lifted her weary head from the small desk where she sat. "When will the pain go away, Lord? Please make it go away." A nagging headache had been plaguing her for hours. She was grateful her workday had finally come to an end. Her last customer, a teenager named Randy, had nearly driven her to distraction. The pimple-faced juvenile had asked for a special designer haircut with the initials *PHS* for Plumers High School cut and shaped into the back of his nearly shaven head. This took extra time of course, which meant she wasn't able to leave the shop until five thirty.

Grabbing her coat and umbrella, Wendy stepped outside. It was snowing hard. A biting wind whipped around her neck, chilling her to the bone. Caught in the current, the umbrella nearly turned inside out. With an exasperated moan, she

snapped it shut. "Can anything else go wrong today?"

Wendy shivered and tromped up the snowy sidewalk toward home. Today had been such an emotional drain. First, Kyle Rogers coming in for a shave and a haircut, which had evoked all sorts of feelings she'd rather not think about. Then another 911 scare, followed by her father's admission of the false calls. After she'd returned to the shop, there had been joke-telling Clyde waiting, then several walk-ins, ending with Randy Olsen, who had just about made her crazy expecting such a ridiculous haircut! It would be so good to get out of her work clothes and into a sweat suit. After she fixed an easy supper of canned soup and grilled cheese sandwiches, she would collapse on the couch for a well-deserved rest. Hopefully, after a good night's sleep, she could come up with a game plan. She needed to figure out something that would keep Dad busy enough so he wouldn't have time to think about her needing a man.

As Wendy approached her house, she noticed there were no lights on inside. She thought that was a bit strange. Dad may not have been able to do many things, but he always managed to have several lights on in the living room.

As usual, the front door was unlocked. Wendy turned the knob and stepped inside. Everything was dark and deathly quiet. Believing Dad to still be asleep in his bedroom, she tiptoed quietly into the living room and nearly tripped over something. She bent down and snapped on a small table lamp.

Wendy let out a startled gasp as the sight of her father came into view. He was lying facedown on the floor, with one bloody hand extended over his head. "Dad! Can you hear me, Dad?" She dropped to her knees and shook his shoulder. "Dear Lord, please let him be okay."

Suddenly Dad turned his head, and his eyes shot open. "Oh, Wendy, I'm so glad you're finally home," he rasped, attempting to roll over.

"What's wrong, Dad?" Wendy's voice shook with fear. "Why are you lying on the floor? What happened to your hand?"

"After my little stunt earlier today, I wanted to make amends," he said, wincing as she helped him roll over and then lifted his hand for inspection. "I was going to make savory stew for dinner, but I'm afraid the knife got the better of me."

"Knife?" she shrieked. "Dad, you know better than to try using a paring knife."

"Actually, it was a butcher knife," he admitted. "I couldn't get my stiff, swollen fingers to work with that little bitty thing you always use."

"So what are you doing on the floor? Did the blood loss make you dizzy?"

He struggled to sit up. "I guess maybe it did."

"Let me get a towel for that hand; then I'll help you get to the couch," Wendy said as she stood up.

"It's a pretty deep cut," her father acknowledged. "I think it might need a few stitches."

"Just stay put until I get back," she insisted.

Wendy returned with a hand towel, which she quickly wrapped around her dad's hand. "Why in the world didn't you

256

call me, or at least call—" She stopped in midsentence. "I guess after our little discussion earlier today, you weren't about to call 911 again, right?"

"Actually, I couldn't call you or the paramedics," he replied with a scowl.

"Why not?" she asked, leaning over so she could help him stand.

"No telephone."

Her head shot up. "No phone! What are you talking about, Dad?"

He nodded toward the phone, sitting on a small table across the room. "I never even considered calling 911 this time, but I did try to call you. The phone seemed to be dead though."

Wendy led him to the couch, then moved to the telephone and picked up the receiver. She frowned. "That's funny. It was working fine when I used it earlier today." Before her father could open his mouth to comment, a light seemed to dawn. "I'll be right back."

"Where are you going?" he called to her retreating form.

"To check the extension in my room."

A few seconds later, Wendy returned to the living room, tears filling her eyes. When she knelt in front of the couch, Dad used his uninjured hand to wipe away the moisture on her cheek. "I'm gonna be okay, honey, so please don't cry."

"The phone was off the hook," she wailed. "How could I have been so careless?" She blinked several times, trying to tame the torrent of tears that seemed to keep on coming. "What if you had bled to death? What if—"

"But I didn't, and I'm going to be fine now that you're here." He gave her a reassuring smile.

"We'd better get you to the hospital. I'm sure that cut will require stitches."

"In a minute," he replied. "First I want to say something."

"What is it, Dad?"

"My actions over the past few weeks have been inexcusable, and I owe you a heartfelt apology, Wendy girl." He grimaced as though he were in pain.

She nodded. "You're forgiven."

"I made those phony calls so you could meet a nice man, but I was meddling," he acknowledged. "Matchmaking and matters of the heart should be left up to the Lord."

"You're the only man I'll ever need," Wendy said softly.

"I'm holding you back," he argued. "If you didn't have to take care of me, you'd probably be married and raising a family of your own by now. If it weren't for my disability, I'm sure you'd be going out on all kinds of dates instead of staying home and playing nurse-maid to a fully grown man."

Wendy shook her head. "I'm not interested in dating—or men, Dad."

"Why the 'I don't like men' attitude?" he pried. "You work on men's hair five days a week. I would think by now one of your customers might have caught your eye."

Wendy moaned. "Remember when I was away at barber's school?"

Her father only nodded in response.

"I dated a guy named Dale Carlson for a while. He treated me awful, Dad."

"Physical abuse?" he asked with raised eyebrows.

She shook her head. "No—uh—he wanted me to compromise my moral standards—if you get my meaning."

"You should have dumped that guy!"

"I didn't have to—he dumped me. When I wouldn't give in to his sexual advances, Mr. Self-Righteous, Phony Christian dropped me for Michelle Stiles."

"I guess I must have had my head in the sand," her father said in obvious surprise. "I didn't know you were that serious about anyone, much less realize some knucklehead was treating you so badly."

"I really didn't want to talk about it," Wendy admitted. "I made up my mind after the Dale fiasco that I was done with men." She shrugged. "So many of the guys who come into the barbershop are either rude, crude, or lewd."

"I understand your feelings of betrayal and hurt," her father said, "but you're not right about your interpretation of all men. One bad apple doesn't have to spoil the whole barrel, you know. You can just pluck out the rotten one and choose a Washington State Delicious."

Wendy smiled at her dad's little pun, then went to the hall closet, where she retrieved his jacket. "The roads are getting bad. I hope it won't take too long to get to the hospital."

"I don't think I'll bleed to death," he said with a sardonic smile. "If I thought it was really serious, I might have you call 911." His forehead wrinkled. "I don't think those paramedics would be too happy to get another call from here today though."

"You're probably right," she agreed. "That older guy didn't respond to you at all like Kyle Rogers, did he?"

"That's putting it mildly. I think he was more than a bit irritated with me for wasting his precious time today."

"Well, just put it out of your head," Wendy said with a smile. "Tonight, *I'm* going to be your rescuer."

The roads weren't quite as bad as Wendy expected, and they made it to the hospital in twenty minutes. Fortunately, there weren't too many emergencies that evening, so Dad was called to an examining room soon after filling out some paperwork.

"Would you like me to go along?" Wendy gave Dad's arm a little squeeze as a young nurse began to usher him away.

He shook his head. "No, I'll be fine. Why don't you go out to the waiting area and try to relax?"

Relax? How on earth was she supposed to relax when her nerves felt taut and her stomach was playing a game of leapfrog? The headache, which she'd acquired around noon, was still pulsating like a jackhammer, too. She would give anything for a cup of hot tea and an aspirin.

Wendy found a chair in the empty waiting room. She rested her elbows on her jean-clad knees and began to methodically rub her forehead. *At least Dad isn't seriously injured, and now that he's agreed to quit playing matchmaker, I don't have to rack my brain to come up with any plan to steer him in some other direction either.*

"What are *you* doing here?"

Wendy jumped at the sound of a deep male voice. Kyle Rogers stood a few feet away, smiling down at her. "Kyle! I— uh—Dad cut his hand."

"Another 911 call?" he asked with raised eyebrows.

She shook her head. "Not this time." She didn't bother telling him about the call her father had placed around noon. If the Grangely grapevine was as active as the one in her small town, then Kyle had probably already heard the whole story from the other paramedics.

"What then?" he asked, taking the seat beside her.

"Dad was trying to make supper, and the knife he was using slipped," she explained. "He has a pretty nasty cut on his left thumb, and it bled quite a lot."

"It's a good thing you were home when it happened."

Wendy blinked several times. "Actually, I wasn't. He did it while I was still at work. I found him lying on the floor."

Kyle grimaced. "You drove him to the hospital yourself?"

"Of course," Wendy replied. "After today, I wasn't about to call 911."

"What happened today?"

Wendy shrugged, realizing he must not have heard anything after all. "It's not important."

She eyed him curiously. "Say, what are *you* doing here, anyway? I thought you were planning to take in a concert tonight. Shouldn't you be there and not here at the hospital?"

He chuckled. "I changed my mind about going. It didn't seem like such a good idea when I thought about attending it alone." He studied Wendy for several seconds, causing her mouth to suddenly go dry. Then he added, "I came here to check on a patient Steve and I brought in yesterday."

I wish he'd quit looking at me like that, she mused. *What are those serious brown eyes of his trying to tell me? How do I know if Kyle is really what he appears to be? I misjudged a so-called Christian once, and I—*

"It was a little boy who'd been mauled by a dog," he said, interrupting her unsettling thoughts.

"What?" Wendy shook her head and shifted restlessly in her chair, trying to force her thoughts back to what Kyle was saying.

"The patient I came to see," he explained. "A five-year-old boy was playing at his neighbor's house and got in the middle of a cat and dog skirmish."

"How awful!" Wendy exclaimed. "Is he going to be all right?"

Kyle nodded. "He'll probably undergo extensive plastic surgery, but I think the little tyke will be fine."

"It's—uh—thoughtful of you to care so much about the patients you bring to the hospital," she stammered. "I think you go over and above the call of duty as a paramedic."

In a surprise gesture, Kyle reached for Wendy's hand. "I do care about my patients, but I also care about you and your father. In fact, I've been thinking that I might stop in and see you both from time to time—when I'm not on duty, that is."

She swallowed hard. "You've been thinking that?"

He nodded. "I really believe your dad could use some company, and since you're so opposed to me playing matchmaker—"

"Don't even go there," she warned.

He shrugged. "Okay, but I could sure use a good barber."

She pulled her hand sharply away. *So that's all he sees me as—just a good barber. In spite of my misgivings, I was actually beginning to think—hope, really—that Kyle was interested in me as a woman, and not merely someone to give him a shave and a haircut. I knew Mr. Perfect Paramedic was too good to be true. He's probably no different than Dale or Gabe after all.*

Just when I'm beginning to make a bit of headway, Wendy pulls into her shell, Kyle thought, letting his head drop into his hands. *What's it going to take to break down her wall of mistrust and get her to open up to me?*

"Dad thinks you're perfect, you know," Wendy blurted out, interrupting his thoughts. "He wants us to get married."

Kyle's head jerked up. "What? Your dad wants *what*?"

"He tried to set us up." Wendy's face contorted. "That's why Dad kept calling 911."

Kyle chewed thoughtfully on his lower lip. "All the calls were phony?"

She nodded. "Every last one of them. He even made a third call around noon today, saying something about feeling dizzy. I thought you might have heard about that one."

He shook his head. "No, I didn't. How do you know he was faking it?"

"He admitted it," she said. "After Steve and Phil left this afternoon, Dad confessed that he'd been trying to play matchmaker all along."

Kyle sucked in a deep breath and expelled it with force. "But today was my day off. I didn't even respond to his 911 call, so—"

"I know," she interrupted. "He was really upset when you didn't show up. That's when I began to get suspicious. Up until then, I just thought he was trying to get attention or simply needed someone to talk to."

Kyle mopped his forehead with the back of his shirtsleeve. "Whew! This is pretty heavy stuff."

She nodded. "My feelings exactly!"

"And here I was trying to come up with some way to fix your dad up with Edna Stone." Kyle shook his head slowly. "Wayne was one step ahead of me all the way, wasn't he?"

"Dad's a pretty slick operator, all right," Wendy admitted. "Guess that's why he did well in business for so many years."

Kyle's eyebrows shot up. "Are you saying that Wayne was dishonest in his business dealings?"

Wendy waved one hand in the air. "No, no, of course not. I just meant—"

"You can see your father now, Miss Campbell," a woman's soft voice interrupted.

Kyle and Wendy both turned to face the nurse who had just entered the waiting room. "Would you like me to go with you?" Kyle asked.

Wendy shook her head. "No, thanks. Dad's my problem,

not yours." She stood up and left the room before Kyle could say another word.

"Oh Lord, what have I gotten myself into?" he moaned.

CHAPTER 7

Over the next several weeks, some drastic changes were made at the Campbell house. Dad no longer spent his time playing matchmaker, which was a welcome relief for Wendy. She was sure it had taken a lot of energy for him to scheme and make those false 911 calls. Even though he'd done it out of love and concern for her, she was glad that whole scenario was behind them. Wendy still got goose bumps every time she heard a siren, but she felt a small sense of peace knowing that if the ambulance should ever go to her house again, it would be for a "real" emergency and not some trumped-up illness.

Another change, which was definitely for the better, was the fact that Dad had asked to go to church again. Wendy, wanting to please her father, was willing to accompany him. She hadn't completely dealt with her feelings of mistrust or

self-doubt, but at least she was being exposed to the Word of God each week. That fact made her feel somewhat better about herself and her circumstances.

True to his word, Kyle Rogers had become a regular visitor, both at the Campbell home and at Wendy's barbershop. A few times Kyle had taken Dad out for a ride in his Bronco and had even made a commitment to see that he would go fishing in the spring—with or without Edna Stone.

"There's no reason your dad can't keep on doing some fun things," Kyle informed Wendy when he stopped by the barbershop one afternoon.

"I doubt that he could even bait his line, much less catch any fish."

"He doesn't have to," Kyle asserted. "I'll do everything for him, and all he will have to do is just sit in a folding chair and hold the pole."

If another customer hadn't come in, Wendy might have debated further. Instead she merely shrugged. "Spring is still a few months away. When the time comes, we'll talk about it."

Kyle flashed her a grin and sauntered out the door.

Wendy frowned. She found his warm smile and kind words unnerving—right along with the verses of scripture he'd quoted on his last few visits. One verse in particular had really set her to thinking. It was Proverbs 29: 25: *"Fear of man will prove to be a snare, but whoever trusts in the Lord is kept safe."* Wendy's trust hadn't been in the Lord for a long time. She wasn't sure she could ever trust again. After the loss of her mother, her father being diagnosed with crippling arthritis, then the episode with Dale, how could she have faith in anyone or anything?

There was also the matter of all the crude, rude men and boys who came into her barbershop. She wasn't a "perfect" Christian by any means, but it was difficult to look past all these men's bad habits and sometimes downright sinful ways. How could she ever believe that any man, except for Dad, could be kind and loving?

"Hey, Wendy, are ya gonna cut my hair or not?"

Jerking her thoughts back to the job at hand, Wendy turned toward the barber's chair. Gabe Hunter was eyeing her curiously. It had only been a few weeks, but the egotistic Romeo was back for another haircut.

He probably came in just to bug me, she grumbled silently. *Well, this time I refuse to let him ruffle my feathers. If he thinks he even has half a chance with me, he's in for a rude awakening!*

Kyle left Wendy's shop feeling more confused than he had in weeks. She seemed interested in the scriptures he'd been sharing with her, and on one occasion had even told him that she and her dad were going to church again. That should have had him singing God's praises. It had been his desire to help both Wendy and Wayne find their way back to the Lord. In a roundabout way, he'd accomplished that, too.

"Then why am I feeling so down?" he vocalized as he headed toward his Bronco.

"You're lonely, Kyle," a little voice nudged. *"You've convinced*

yourself that there is no room for love or romance in your heart. You're not trusting Me in all areas of your life either."

"What do you want me to do, Lord—ask Wendy on a date?"

No answer. That still, small voice seemed to have vanished as quickly as it had come. Kyle scratched the back of his head and grimaced. He needed time to think. He needed time to pray about this. A drive up to Plumers Pond sure seemed to be in order.

"You've got a phone call," Dad announced as he hobbled into the kitchen where Wendy was cooking.

"Who is it? Can you take a message? Supper's almost ready, and—"

"It's Kyle," her father said with a smirk.

Wendy turned the stove down, put a lid on the spaghetti sauce, and headed for the living room. "Hello, Kyle," she said into the phone. "What's up?"

"I—uh," Kyle stammered.

"You sound kind of nervous."

"Yeah, I guess I am."

"Well, you needn't be. I don't bite, you know." She chuckled. "Some of my customers might think I am pretty *cutting*, though."

Kyle laughed at her pun, which seemed to put him at ease. "Listen, the reason I'm calling is, I was up at Plumers Pond today, and it's still frozen solid."

"I'm not surprised," Wendy replied. "It's been a drawn-out, cold winter, and I'm beginning to wonder if spring will ever get here." There was a long pause, which left her wondering if maybe Kyle had hung up. "Are you still there, Kyle?"

"Yeah, I'm here," he said with a small laugh. "I was just trying to get up enough nerve to ask if you'd like to go ice-skating with me on Saturday night."

"Ice-skating?" she echoed.

"I just found out that the singles' group from my church is going out to the pond for a skating party. I thought it might be kind of fun, and I'd really like it if you went along."

Wendy's mind whirled. Was this a date he was asking her on? Not Kyle dropping by the barbershop for a short visit. Not Dad and her going to a Christian concert—but just the two of them, skating with a bunch of other people their own age. She did enjoy Kyle's company; there was no denying it. In all the times she'd seen him, he'd never once said an unkind thing or done anything to make her think he was anything less than the Christian he professed to be. Still—

"Now it's my turn to ask. Are you there?" Kyle's deep voice cut into her troubling thoughts.

"Yes, I'm here," she said in a trembling voice. "I was just taken by surprise, that's all."

"Surprised that I ice-skate, or that I'm asking you out on a date?"

So it was a real date then. Kyle had just said as much. Now her only problem was deciding whether to accept or not. Wendy hadn't been on a date since she and Dale broke up.

Could she really start dating after all this time? Could she trust Kyle not to break her heart the way Dale had? Of course, that could easily be avoided by simply not allowing herself to become romantically involved again.

"How about it, Wendy?" Kyle asked, invading her thoughts once more. "Can I pick you up around seven Saturday evening?"

Wendy licked her lips and swallowed hard. She opened her mouth to decline, but to her surprise, she said, "Sure, why not?"

"Great!" Kyle said enthusiastically. "See you soon."

Wendy hung up the phone and dropped onto the couch with a groan. "Now why in the world did I say yes?"

Being with Kyle and the other young people turned out to be more fun than Wendy expected.

"You're a good skater," Kyle said, skidding to a stop in front of Wendy, nearly causing her to lose her balance.

"You're not so bad yourself," she shot back.

"Are you having fun?" He pivoted so he could skate beside her.

She nodded. "It's been years since I've been on skates. I wasn't sure I could even stand up on these skinny little blades, much less make it all the way around the frozen pond."

"How about taking a break?" Kyle suggested. "One of the guys has started a bonfire. We've got lots of hot dogs and marshmallows to roast."

"I admit, I am kind of hungry. Guess all this cold, fresh air has given me an appetite."

"Yeah, me, too. Of course, I could eat anytime. While I was growing up in Northern California, Mom used to say all three of us boys could eat her out of house and home."

Wendy giggled. "So is a voracious appetite your worst sin?"

He eyed her curiously. "You're kidding, right?"

She shook her head and reached up to slip her fuzzy blue earmuffs back in place. "You seem so nice—almost perfect. Dad thinks you're about the best thing to happen since the invention of homemade ice cream."

"Whoa!" Kyle raised one gloved hand. "I don't even come close to being perfect. I may strive to be more like Jesus; but like any other human being, perfectionism is something I'll sure never know."

Wendy shrugged. "Maybe I expect too much from people. Dad says I do anyway."

"Part of living the Christian life is being willing to accept others just as they are, Wendy."

Kyle reached for her hand.

Even though they both wore gloves, she could feel the warmth of his touch. It caused her heart to skip a few beats. Kyle's serious, dark eyes seemed to be challenging her to let go of the past and forgive those who had hurt her. She wanted so badly to believe Kyle was different from Dale or any of the guys who came into the barbershop, wanting more than she was willing to give. How good it would feel to accept folks for who they were and quit looking for perfection. Most importantly, Wendy would have to learn to trust again, and

that frightened her. She might be able to trust the Lord, but trusting another man would put her in a vulnerable position. Wendy wasn't sure she could risk being hurt again.

The ride back to town was a quiet one. Both Wendy and Kyle seemed absorbed in their own private thoughts. Only the pleasant strain of Steve Green's mellow voice singing "My Soul Found Rest" filled the interior of Kyle's Bronco. Wendy struggled with tears that threatened to spill over. She wondered if her soul would ever find rest amid the turmoil of life.

"This is my favorite CD," Kyle said, breaking the silence between them. "Steve Green has so many good songs. I always feel as though the Lord is speaking to my heart when I listen to contemporary Christian music."

Wendy could only nod. She didn't want to admit it to Kyle, but she rarely ever listened to any type of music. In fact, some music actually grated on her nerves, but the song that played now had a serene effect on her. She was beginning to think maybe she should start playing some Christian music in her shop. *That might even deter some of the crude lumberjacks from telling all their lewd jokes and wisecracks,* she mused.

"I'll bet someone could even get saved listening to Christian music like what's on this CD," Wendy said, hardly realizing she'd spoken her thoughts out loud.

"I think you're right," Kyle agreed. "In fact, some of the teens at my church found Christ at a Christian rock concert not so long ago."

Wendy frowned. "I've been a Christian since I was a child, but I strayed from God a few years ago." She had absolutely no idea why she was telling Kyle all this, but the words seemed to keep tumbling out. "After a bad relationship with a so-called Christian, I was terribly hurt and started to get bitter about certain things." When Kyle remained quiet, she added solemnly, "God could have kept it from happening, you know."

"God doesn't always make things go away just so we will have it easy," Kyle put in. "Part of growing in our Christian walk is learning how to cope with life's problems and letting Christ carry our burdens when the load is too heavy for us."

"I don't do too well in the trusting department either," Wendy admitted, leaning back in the seat and closing her eyes.

"Who don't you trust?" Kyle glanced over at her with a look of concern.

"Men," she announced. "I don't trust men."

Kyle's forehead wrinkled. "Not even your dad?"

She opened her eyes and shrugged. "Until he started making false 911 calls, I had always trusted Dad implicitly."

"But he really feels bad about all that and has promised it will never happen again," Kyle reminded. "Just last week, when I took him for a ride up to Plumers Creek, Wayne told me how guilty he felt for telling all those lies." He reached over to pat Wendy's hand. "Your dad's a Christian, but he's not perfect either. Like I was telling you earlier tonight, we all make mistakes. It's what we do about our blunders that really counts."

"I think I can trust Dad again," Wendy said thoughtfully.

"It's other men that give me a problem."

Kyle grew serious. "Other men, like me?"

She laughed nervously. "You get paid to be trustworthy."

"I'm not always working though," he reminded. "I have to try to be a Christian example whether I'm administering first aid to an accident victim or teaching a sixth-grade Sunday school class full of unruly boys."

"You teach Sunday school?" she asked in surprise.

He nodded. "Yep, every other week—on the Sundays when I'm not scheduled for duty. Sometimes those rowdy kids are enough to put anyone's Christianity to the test."

Wendy thought about the hyperactive, undisciplined kids who came into the barbershop. They needed to be shown the love of Jesus, too. There had to be a better way to deal with her customers than merely pretending to be friendly, or snapping back at guys like Gabe. At that moment, Wendy resolved in her heart to find out what it was.

CHAPTER 3

Wendy brought her Bible to the shop to read during lulls. If she was going to find a better way to deal with the irritation she felt with some of her customers, she knew the answer would be found in the scriptures. She also planned to buy a few Christian CDs so she could play them at work—both for her own benefit as well as the clientele's.

Today was a cold, blustery Tuesday, and she'd only had two customers so far. She didn't really mind though, because it was another opportunity to get into God's Word. She grabbed an apple from the fruit bowl on the counter, dropped into her barber's chair, and randomly opened the Bible to the book of Matthew.

Chapter 7 dealt with the subject of judging others. Wendy was reminded that instead of searching for sawdust in someone

else's eyes, she should be examining her own life and looking for the plank that would no doubt be there, in the form of her own sin. She chewed thoughtfully on the Red Delicious apple and let the Holy Spirit speak to her heart. Instead of enjoying the unique variety of people who frequented her shop, she'd been judging them. Rather than allowing herself to get a kick out of the clean jokes and witnessing about the Lord to those who told off-color puns, she'd been telling herself that all men were bad. Even though Kyle Rogers had made an impression on her with his tenderness, patience, and kind words, Wendy had questioned his motives. This was judging. There was no getting around it, and according to God's Word, Wendy was no better than the worst of all sinners. If she didn't get herself right with the Lord, she, too, would be judged.

Without a moment's hesitation, she knew what she must do. Wendy bowed her head and prayed fervently, "Father, please forgive me for my negative, condemning attitude. Heal me of the hurt deep in my heart, and help me learn to love others just as You do. Help me to trust You and become a witness of Your love and grace." A small sob escaped her lips. "And if Kyle Rogers is the man you want me to love and trust, then please give me some sign." When she finished her heartfelt prayer, Wendy opened her eyes. For the first time since her broken relationship with Dale Carlson, she felt a sense of peace flood her soul. She was released from all the pain of the past and knew that with God's help, she could finally be a witness for Him.

Wendy glanced out the front window and caught sight of

Harvey, the mailman, slipping some mail into the box outside the shop. She stepped down from the chair. Taking one more bite of the crisp, juicy apple, she headed outside, not even bothering with a coat.

Kyle was just rounding the corner, heading up the street toward Campbell's Barbershop, when he saw Wendy come out the front door. His mouth curved into a smile. He hadn't seen her since their date last Saturday night. He could only hope that she'd be as glad to see him as he was to see her now.

Kyle had spent most of the weekend thinking about Wendy and the way she made him feel. His resolve not to get romantically involved with any woman was quickly fading, and he seemed powerless to stop it. He'd read the scriptures and prayed until there were no more words. He'd petitioned God to show him some sign that Wendy might be able to respond to his love. He didn't have a clue what it might be, but just the same, he'd made up his mind to come to the shop today and have a heart-to-heart talk with Wendy. If she would agree to at least give their relationship a chance, then he was going to trust God to work out all the details that seemed impossible to him. After all, if he was really trying to do the things Jesus would do, it wasn't his right to make decisions about the future. Fear that his job would get in the way of love or marriage could no longer be an issue.

Kyle watched in fascination as petite little Wendy, wearing only a pair of blue jeans and a long-sleeved blouse, covered

with a green smock, reached into the mailbox. It was a cold day, and there was still snow on the ground. The sidewalk appeared slick, like the frozen pond, with ice glistening in the sun's golden rays. Kyle was about to call out for her to be careful when the unthinkable happened. Just like an ice skater who'd lost her balance, Wendy's body swayed first to one side, then the other. Her feet slipped and slid while she tried hopelessly to regain her balance. There seemed to be nothing Kyle could do but stand there and watch as beautiful little Wendy went down, landing hard on her back and hitting her head against the icy, cold sidewalk.

Doing a fair share of slipping and sliding himself, Kyle raced down the sidewalk to Wendy's aid. When he discovered that she wasn't conscious, his paramedic skills kicked in. From the evidence of the apple core lying nearby, Kyle was quite sure Wendy not only had the wind knocked out of her, but was probably asphyxiating on a piece of that apple. He knew what he had to do, and it must be done quickly, or she would choke to death.

Kyle positioned her head and knelt closer. *Look, listen, feel for air. . . .* His training ran through his mind.

Nothing!

He repositioned her jaw again, but to no avail. When he tried to give her mouth-to-mouth, it didn't work. Everything confirmed his worst suspicions: a small piece of the offending fruit must be stuck in her throat. He went into immediate action and was able to dislodge it using the Heimlich maneuver. His initial burst of praise and elation faded at once when Wendy still didn't breathe on her own. Fearful for her life, yet relying on his faith, he began mouth-to-mouth resuscitation again.

Breathe, Wendy honey. . . . God, please make her breathe. . . .

Though she started breathing, she still didn't regain consciousness. "Wake up, beautiful lady. I haven't told you what I came to say." Kyle quickly examined her to be sure nothing was injured. He prayed earnestly, "Oh Lord, this is not the way I planned for things to be. I had a whole speech prepared for Wendy, and now I may never get the chance to say what's on my mind. Please, Lord—let her be all right."

Wendy's eyelids popped open. Someone's lips had been touching hers. They were soft and warm. She thought she'd heard a voice. Had someone called her *beautiful*? Kyle stared down at her with a look of love and concern etched on his handsome face. Where was she, and why was he leaning over her? She was sure she must be dreaming.

"Wh–what happened?"

"I was coming to your shop so I could talk to you about something very important," Kyle explained, gently stroking the side of her face. He leaned closer and kissed her forehead, his tears falling to her cheeks. "I saw you slip and fall on the ice. You choked on that apple." He pointed to the small piece, just a few feet away. "Thank God you're alive!"

"I was just finishing the apple when I walked outside to get the mail. I—I—"

Kyle placed one finger against her lips. "Shh. . . Don't try to talk right now." He probed the back of her head gently with his fingers. "As amazing as this may seem, there's not even a lump. Does your head hurt anywhere?"

She smiled up at him, tears gathering in her own eyes. "No, not really. I think I just had the wind knocked out of me."

"You looked so helpless and beautiful—just like Snow White, lying there beside that Red Delicious," Kyle said with a catch in his voice. "Only your apple wasn't poison, and I thank God you responded to the Heimlich maneuver, then mouth-to-mouth resuscitation so quickly."

"Mouth-to-mouth?" she echoed, bringing her fingers up to lightly touch her lips. "At first I thought I was dreaming. Then I opened my eyes and thought I'd been kissed by a very handsome man." A shiver ran up her spine, and she knew it was not from the cold. "And you must be Prince Charming, who came along and rescued me."

He nodded. "I know God sent me here today, but I sure didn't think I'd be playing the part of a paramedic on my day off."

She smiled up at him. "You've rescued me from a whole lot more than a fall to the ice and an apple stuck in my throat."

"Really? What else have I rescued you from?" Kyle asked, never taking his eyes off her smiling face.

She swallowed hard. "Your kindness, patience, and biblical counseling have all helped. I was reading my Bible right before I came outside, and God's Word confirmed everything you've been trying to tell me."

"I'm so glad," he said sincerely.

"Thanks for saving me," she whispered as she sat up. "I—I probably shouldn't be saying this, but I think I might be falling in love with you."

"You took the words right out of my mouth." He bent his head down to capture her mouth in a kiss so sweet it took her breath away.

"Oh, Kyle," she murmured when their lips finally separated, "if you keep that up, I might be forced to call 911."

He laughed heartily. "Guess I'd better get you inside to the phone, then, because now that God has finally kicked some sense into my stubborn head, I'm liable to keep kissing you all day long."

Wendy drew in a deep breath and leaned her head against his strong shoulder. As they entered the barbershop a few moments later, she murmured, "Thank You, Lord. I think I can learn to trust both You and Kyle now." Her flushed cheeks dimpled as she smiled. "And thank you, Dad—our match-maker 911."

About the Author

Wanda E. Brunstetter is a bestselling author who enjoys writing Amish-themed as well as contemporary and historical novels. Descended from Anabaptists herself, Wanda became deeply interested in the Plain People when she married her husband, Richard, who grew up in a Mennonite church in Pennsylvania. Wanda and her husband live in Washington State but take every opportunity to visit their Amish friends in various communities across the country, gathering further information about the Amish way of life.

Wanda and her husband have two grown children and six grandchildren. In her spare time, Wanda enjoys photography, ventriloquism, gardening, reading, stamping, and having fun with her family.

In addition to her novels, Wanda has written Amish cookbooks, Amish devotionals, and several Amish children's books as well as numerous novellas, stories, articles, poems, and puppet scripts.

Visit Wanda's website at www.wandabrunstetter.com and feel free to e-mail her at wanda@wandabrunstetter.com.